FAE RISING

BOOK FOUR IN THE FAE BLOODLINES SERIES

ROSE GARCIA

For Jessica R.

Thank you for sticking with me from the beginning!

THE FAE REALM OF
FAEVENLY

TORCH
LAKE

STRONG
HAVEN EAST

MOTHER
OF RIVERS

SUMMIT
RANGE

SAND
BLUFF

GREEN
FALLS

THE
GREAT
COVE

THE MORNING SEA

1

GABRIELA

The carriage lurched forward with a jerk, creaking and crunching over the gravel road before settling into a steady rhythm as the horses pulled us away from Strong Haven palace. We weren't just leaving—we were fleeing.

With my eyes fixed on the view, I studied the massive gold-and-ivory structure with its magnificent spires as we rolled past, my heart in my throat as it disappeared from sight. Because once we left, there was no going back.

My mother was born there, and I had been visiting the palace since I was little. I had combed the marble-lined hallways, hidden in the thick trees and brush in the gardens, and even daringly made my way across the roofline once, though my parents didn't know, of course.

Now, Strong Haven was evacuating in waves, with my carriage and five others in the first group because every province—except for the Sublands, where we were headed—wanted us dead.

And so did Draven the Witch.

He had escaped the dungeon of Strong Haven

palace after twenty years of imprisonment and was helped by Leaf, the fae protector who had my heart. Leaf had even given Draven the last remaining aquoise stone we had been searching for, though deep down I couldn't believe he acted willingly. There was no way he would've turned on me and Strong Haven like that.

Not after what we had shared. Not after everything he meant to me.

With the stone, Draven's powers would know no bounds. I didn't know how any of us could survive what he had planned.

But the thing that hurt most was a loss that cut so deep, I didn't think I'd ever recover. My mom was dead, and my dad had decided to stay with her in the Passing Place.

Wrapping my arms around my waist, I eased myself away from the window and settled back against the smooth purple velvet seat, shifting my gaze to my boots that poked out from under my brown silk dress. Images of the Passing Place filled my mind—the lush lavender field, the apple trees bursting with shiny red fruit, the creek where I had seen my mother with the skirt of her dress tied at her knees, fishing. She had no idea she was dead. Her mind somehow shielding her from the truth, making her believe all was well and she was merely enjoying a long visit to Faevenly with my dad.

I supposed being in that state was better than the alternative.

My uncle Manny sat next to me, and across from

him sat Lady Sonia, the palace healer. They didn't know about my mom and dad, because I had found out only minutes before getting in the carriage. I needed to tell them but didn't think I could manage a conversation about it just yet. I needed a moment to gather myself.

"All will be well, Gabriela," Lady Sonia offered in her soothing voice. "You will see."

She wore her long dark hair pulled up in a loose bun, and had on a long gray dress. There was much I admired about Lady Sonia, including her unwavering optimism. But with everything that had happened, and all that was still left to face, I knew she was wrong. Nothing would be well. Not ever.

"I don't know, Sonia," Uncle Manny muttered.

I pulled my gaze up from my shoes and studied him. He wasn't my blood uncle, but was my dad's best friend since forever. So he was just like family. He sat with his slim frame slightly hunched over. He wore a fae outfit of dark green pants and a long-sleeved brown shirt, his jeans and shirt from the human realm undoubtedly shoved in his bag like my jeans and my shirt were shoved in mine. He had been in Faevenly with my mom and dad before I was born, and together they had gone through some serious dangers. If what we were going through now was worse than what they had gone through then, we were really screwed.

"Now is not the time for such thoughts, Manny," Lady Sonia said in a somewhat terse tone.

Uncle Manny rubbed his stubbled face, then

combed his fingers through his thick black hair that was beginning to show gray along the edges. "You're right, Sonia," he blew out. Then he reached out and patted my knee. "Sorry, *mija*. I'll do better."

"It's okay, Uncle Manny," I said, placing my hand over his and giving it a squeeze. "You don't have to apologize."

Uncle Manny's usual playful and cheery style had been all but erased and was replaced with despair and grief. The transformation was unnerving, to say the least, because I had never really seen him like this. Telling him about my mom and dad might push him over the edge. But still, he needed to know. They all did.

"Thank you, *mija*," he muttered.

The carriage dipped, then jostled back up. I tightened my grip around Manny's hand as I kept myself from sliding off my seat.

He steadied my arms with a smile. "Feels like the potholes in the roads back home."

Recognizing his attempt at trying to make me feel better, I forced a smile in return. "It does."

The carriage resumed a steady pace again, and my uncle let out a chuckle. "Hey, remember that time you hit that pothole so hard you got a flat tire?"

I smiled, because that was one of my favorite memories with him. "Of course I remember. I called you crying and you came over and fixed it and I got back home without my parents even knowing."

"Yep, and what did we do before you went home?"

"You took me for ice cream."

He turned to Lady Sonia. "Not just any ice cream. It was the world famous Amy's ice cream way on the other side of town. We also got brownies."

"Yep," I said, recalling the cool and creamy chocolate chip cookie dough ice cream dolloped on top of a chewy fudge brownie. "We sure did."

We laughed a bit more before a quiet lull returned to the cabin, my gaze drifting to the passing trees outside the carriage. As hard as I tried not to think about them, my thoughts went back to my mom and dad. Mom looked so happy in the Passing Place, and I wondered how long it would take for her to figure out she was dead. I couldn't blame my dad at all for wanting to stay with her as long as possible. If it were me, I'd probably do the same. But if things got worse in Faevenly, which I was sure they would, then I'd need to get him. And he'd have to tell her.

I folded my hands on my lap with my heart shattered and my spirit lower than low. I was grateful to have Uncle Manny with me, and I really hated not telling him about my mom and dad, but I wasn't ready. It was almost as if keeping the information to myself made it less real. Which was a really dumb way of looking at things, but I couldn't help it.

"You can tell us, Gabriela," Lady Sonia said in a half whisper. Her hand rested on her necklace with an opal stone. She had worn that necklace for as long as I could remember. Most times, she wore it tucked under her clothing. Other times, she wore it out. Like today.

Uncle Manny's back stiffened as he sat straight. He looked from me to Lady Sonia and then back to me. "Is there something you need to tell us, *mija*?"

I swallowed. Of course Lady Sonia would know I needed to tell them something. She was the palace healer, was hundreds of years old, and had powers I couldn't even understand. When I was little, I made a game of looking for her and her healing chamber whenever I visited.

Once, I found her chamber behind a hidden door in the grand hall, another time at the top of a stairwell I had discovered in the back of the palace—a stairwell I had only seen that day and never again. But the strangest place was in a glass dome deep in the garden surrounded by flowering bushes.

I had spent hours with Lady Sonia, learning about herbs and tinctures, following her around and asking her tons of questions. I wished I had never stopped visiting and that I remembered the stuff she had taught me, but understood my parents' desire to keep me away from Faevenly because they thought it was safer that way. Now that I knew how a group of fae had tried to kill me in our bakery when I was little, I understood.

"Well," I said, clearing my throat, "there is something I need to tell y'all, something I found out before we left the palace. Something about my mom and dad." I shifted in my seat as a lump formed in my throat and my eyes filled with tears. I drew in a long deep breath, forcing myself to keep it together because the last thing I wanted was to be weak.

"Go ahead, *mija*," Uncle Manny soothed.

With a nod, I said, "Well, after I finished packing my things in my room, before we left Faevenly, Maid Gidna left me by myself for a while. An overwhelming need to see my dad and find out where my mom was overcame me, because I didn't know for sure if she was with him. So I used my Avila witchy skills to go to the Passing Place."

A stream of sunlight filtered in through the carriage opening, casting a ray of light over Lady Sonia's smooth ivory face and showcasing her sparkling hazel eyes that sometimes looked blue. She had thick, long lashes and her eyes blinked with surprise. She wasn't expecting me to say that.

"Did you see him?" she asked.

"I did. I was telling him about Leaf and the aquoise, when he helped me realize something." I paused for a few long seconds, remembering how I had wrapped my arms around him when I realized he was alive. "My dad isn't actually dead."

Manny's eyes widened and his mouth fell open. "What? Your dad is alive?"

"Yes, he's alive."

Manny stayed so still I thought he had stopped breathing. "Are you sure?" he asked.

I nodded. "Absolutely sure."

He stared at me with a large smile. "Thank you, Jesus!" he exclaimed, making the sign of the cross up and down his body and side to side. "And your mom?"

Fresh pain shot through my heart as I looked down and moved my head from side to side.

"Oh, *mija*," Uncle Manny said. He reached over and wrapped his arms around me. "My dear girl."

Tears spilled from my eyes as I clutched him to me, feeling grateful to have him with me especially since he had always been with me. He was at the hospital when I was born, and he came over and visited and babysat all the time when I was little. He never missed a birthday, or any of my church milestones like my baptism and confirmation. And he always seemed to be the loudest one cheering at my fencing matches.

Lady Sonia patted my back, then reached out with a handkerchief. I took the white silk fabric and wiped my cheeks.

"Gabriela," she said after giving me a few moments. "I am relieved to hear about your father, but am saddened to hear about your mother. So very saddened." She tilted her head a little. "But what is Lord Julio's plan? Why is he there, if he is alive?"

I drew in a breath and sat up. "My mom doesn't know she's dead, and my dad can't leave her. Not yet, anyway."

Uncle Manny sat back, speechless. Lady Sonia kept quiet too. The carriage jostled again, but this time it came to a stop.

Uncle Manny peered out the window. "What's going on?"

I was turning to look when Lady Sonia leaned

forward and took my hand. "Gabriela, tell no one your father is alive. Understand?"

Her words surprised me. "What?" I flashed Uncle Manny a look. He appeared as confused as me.

"What do you mean, Sonia?" he asked.

The sound of horses whinnying and people shouting filled the air, and a tingle of panic raced across my spine.

"Lord Julio is important. We must do whatever is necessary to keep him safe." She scooted closer to us and said in a low voice, "I sense he has a great role still to play in all this."

Uncle Manny blinked. "A great role? Like what?"

"I am unsure. It is a feeling inside of me that has been growing for a while now. A feeling I cannot explain."

Her words filled me with hope, because I desperately needed my dad. With a swallow, I nodded. "I won't say anything."

"Neither will I," Uncle Manny added.

A guard dashed into place against the carriage, his bow out and arrow nocked. Whatever was happening looked serious, and a blast of fear shot through me.

"Hey, what's going on?" Uncle Manny asked.

Keeping his attention on the woods, the guard replied, "Someone has been spotted on the road. Lord Rook fears they mean ill. He and a team are scouting the area."

Uncle Manny ran his fingers through his hair. "Of

course there's someone out there who means ill," he muttered. "This is Faevenly, after all."

The horses stamped nervously, the carriage rocking beneath us. No one moved. Even the air felt suspended—thick with pine and tension, every breath sharp against my lungs. I strained to hear anything beyond the creak of wood and the distant hum of insects. Nothing. Just waiting.

Eying the guard, I told myself it was precaution, but my pulse betrayed me. If the provinces had truly turned, then danger wasn't closing in—it was already here.

And we were completely exposed.

2

GABRIELA

My hand flew to my back, searching for my fighting stick—but came up empty. Panic surged through me. If someone was out there, I needed it. And not just because it was a weapon. Leaf had given it to me.

"What is it?" Manny asked.

"My fighting stick. I don't have it."

My mind raced through the events of the last few days, trying to visualize the last time I had my stick. I didn't have it at my house when I fought Leaf because I grabbed a fighting stick by my front door before I rushed him. That left the bakery and the confrontation with Draven. That was the last place I remembered having it.

I shuddered at the thought of Draven and how close he had been to me. I was pretty sure I had my stick with me while I was there, but the entire sequence of events was muddled and the details lost to me. But according to Leaf, I had tapped into my Avila witchy skills to drive Draven away and in the process brought my *abuela* back to life. And then I passed out.

I must've left it there.

Maybe Maid Gidna had stuffed a weapon inside my bag. My eyes darted around the carriage, searching for my things.

Lady Sonia rested her hand on my knee. "Your things are stored in a different carriage. Besides, I do not sense you need a weapon. Not this time." Her words should have comforted me. They didn't.

The last time I traveled with her in a carriage, we were with Uncle Leto, Leaf, and a handful of guards. We were traveling to Strong Haven West to persuade the members of the Council of Six to support me as the head of Strong Haven and head of Faevenly in an effort to prevent the Kane family from coming into power, because having them in power meant having Draven in power. But on our way, we were attacked and I ended up charging out of the carriage with my fighting stick and battling side by side with Leaf.

We were able to fend off our attackers that day, and it was in large part because of Leaf's fighting skills. But then he had to go and break Alexander's neck, killing him on the spot. Which was why the provinces wanted us dead, and why we were fleeing Strong Haven.

"Gabriela," Lady Sonia said, "do you sense any impending peril?"

There were things I could do, like my dad and my *abuela*. I could see and communicate with spirits, and I could sense danger. Sometimes it was a subtle tingle at the back of my neck that told me something was wrong. Other times it was a hard vibration that raced through my body. I inherited the ability from my dad's family, and it was only becoming a bigger part of me now that I had been in Faevenly.

Ever since everything started happening, a warning tingle had been a constant. So much so, I hardly even recognized it anymore. But if I focused, I thought I might be able to sense beyond it.

"I don't know. But I can try," I said.

Forcing myself to relax, I closed my eyes and turned my attention to my neck, my jaw, my forehead, even my shoulders and arms. Everything felt... normal. Or at least, my new normal. Did that mean whoever was out there was harmless?

"Do you sense anything?" Lady Sonia asked again.

Opening my eyes, I said, "Well, I've felt a constant low tingle since I was attacked at my school back in the human realm, but right now I don't feel anything beyond that."

Uncle Manny was quick to express his caution. "Um, is that a good thing?"

"I think so." I glanced out the window, past the guard, and surveyed the brush and the trees. The sun shone brightly through the tall pines as the fresh air wafted through the carriage. By any standard, it was a gorgeous day, and everything seemed okay. I took that as a good sign.

"I think we should go see for ourselves," I said.

Uncle Manny raised his brow. "I don't know if that's the wisest thing to do right now."

I wrapped my fingers around the door handle. "I

don't know either. But I feel like it's what we should do." Even if it was a mistake.

Manny looked to Sonia for a response. She nodded slightly, signaling her agreement with my plan. "Let us go see."

I opened the door and we climbed out. We had been traveling for hours, and my legs were stiff and achy. Even with the velvet-covered seats, my backside was killing me.

"You should not be out of the carriage," the guard warned as he stepped aside.

"It'll be fine," I assured him.

I walked around in a small circle, stretching my legs and studying the area. We were on a narrow dirt road. Carriages were ahead of ours, and behind as well, leaving ours in the middle. Guards were standing around, their bows and arrows still in their hands and pointed in every direction.

Up at the front of the convoy, I spotted Rook marching our way. The tall, muscular fae from the Sublands was unlike any fae I had seen in Faevenly. And honestly, I had no idea what to make of him, but he was a trusted ally to my mom and dad and my Uncle Leto. He was also very close to Leaf.

"My Queen," he said with a stern nod. "You must stay in your carriage until we know what is afoot."

"Why? What's going on?" I asked, dismissing his command, still thinking it sounded so odd to be called queen.

"Yeah, what's happening?" Uncle Manny asked.

Rook's thick brows furrowed, as if bothered by our questioning. "There are footprints up ahead on the road. My scouts are combing the area."

"Footprints?" I looked at the road again. It was made of tightly packed stones with a thin layer of dirt on top. Even though no one else was on the road, I imagined others used it from time to time. "But this is a road. Aren't footprints expected?"

"Yes, but these veered off into the woods. And are fresh. Someone is attempting to avoid detection."

"Oh," I said in a whisper, taking in our surroundings with newfound fear. Someone knew we were coming.

A rustling in the brush cut through the air. Rook swung his arm out, sweeping me behind him. He lifted his fisted hand in the air. The guards directed their aim in the direction of the sound and held steady while Rook stepped forward.

"Hark!" he called out in his deep voice, his hand still raised while his other one pulled a dagger from his belt. "Come forth now and your life will be spared from certain death!"

The brush and trees were thick, forcing me to squint as I searched for a glimpse of who or what was in the woods, my mind jumping straight to Draven. Was the deadly soul-sucking fae witch coming to kill us once and for all? With the aquoise in his possession, he could easily do it.

Rook advanced another step. "My guards will fire their arrows if you do not comply!"

The guards held their bows high and their arrows taut, ready to unleash on command. Rook opened his fisted hand. Before he could move his hand again, a small voice called out, "We are coming!"

Another added, "Do not harm us!"

Rook held his position for a few seconds, then lowered his hand and sheathed his dagger. The guards followed his lead.

Leaves crunched and twigs snapped. The sounds grew closer while whoever had spoken made their way out of the woods and toward the road. Two small and slender fae emerged. Not enemies. Not soldiers.

"Adva and Aedon," Lady Sonia said, advancing toward them with a smile. "Thank the sun, the moon, and the stars you two are alive. I thought you both had perished long ago."

"We have not, my lady," the young girl said.

"We are alive and well," the young boy added, "living in peace in the forest."

Lady Sonia offered a quick introduction. "Rook, Lady Gabriela, Manny, these are brother and sister Adva and Aedon. They are, or were, longtime servants to House Strong. They have not been seen since Princess Celyse and Lord Julio left Faevenly for the human realm so many years ago." She smiled at them. "I am most pleased to see them well."

The pair bowed low. "Thank you, Lady Sonia. We are pleased to see you as well," they said together.

Rook surveyed them for a moment before asking, "Is the forest safe?"

"Yes, Lord Rook," Adva answered. "It is safe here."

"Good," Rook nodded.

Rook directed his attention to the skies. The bright day was growing dark as the sun made its descent and the faint view of a full moon was making its appearance. He frowned, looking displeased with having to stop earlier than he wanted.

"We will camp here tonight," he grumbled. Then he called out, "Move the carriages into position for the night!"

A burst of activity unleashed as he returned back to the front of the caravan. I should've kept track of our carriage, but I couldn't. I was too busy staring at the doe-eyed, brown haired fae siblings.

They knew my mom and dad. And they might have answers.

Before I could ask them anything, the bustle of making camp for the night pulled me away. A team tended to the horses. Another team set up campfires inside the tree line in an open area perfect for setting up for the night. My team, which included Maid Gidna, Uncle Manny, Lady Sonia, and the two small fae, set about arranging an area for sleeping and another area for cooking.

By the time everyone finished their tasks, the sun had long gone and a multitude of brilliant stars scattered across the velvety dark blue sky alongside the brightest moon I'd ever seen. Lady Sonia ushered me and Manny to a roaring fire, where Rook and two guards were standing. Thick logs circled the flames like benches.

Uncle Manny and I sat on one log, and Lady Sonia sat on another. Rook excused himself from the guards and sat across from us. I didn't notice a large sack near Rook's log until he lifted it up. He rifled through it and brought out a small brown packet tied with string.

"Bread," he said, passing it around. "Everyone take one."

The sack made its way around. I took my bread out when it got to me. When it got to Uncle Manny, he held it for a while then said to Rook. "Can I trade this for a couple of hot dogs?"

He laughed, and even though I didn't want to laugh, I couldn't help myself. Rook kept his serious expression, not looking at all amused.

"Nevermind, Rook," Uncle Manny said quickly. "This will do."

He smiled at me, as if we were at a normal cookout and not fleeing for our lives, then tapped his packet against mine.

"*Buen provecho*, Gabriela."

"*Buen provecho*, Uncle Manny."

I untied the string, then unfolded the paper, exposing a thin piece of wheat bread with seeds and bits of fruit. I took a bite, and a delicious burst of spiciness filled my mouth along with crunchy nuts that tasted like walnuts and savory tartness that tasted like cranberries. The bread instantly reminded me of something my mother would have made, and a sharp pang of sadness descended on me. And just like that, she was gone all over again. My uncle must have sensed my thoughts because he moved in closer to me in that reassuring way of his.

"It will be okay," he said in a low voice.

Even though I didn't feel the same way, I nodded. "I know."

While everyone ate in silence, I kept a keen eye on everything around me. Three similar-sized fires roared nearby—one for the guards, or the guards who weren't patrolling, and the other two for the ladies and servants of Strong Haven. Adva and Aedon were nowhere to be seen. I assumed they had gone back to wherever they lived.

After a while, Lady Sonia broke the silence. "This bread is called fruit flats. It is often prepared for long journeys like ours and is most popular in Faevenly." She held it up. "A small piece like this provides great sustenance."

Staring at the bread, I thought of all the things I didn't know about the fae realm. Like this bread. I studied the crispiness, eyeing the bits of nuts and fruit. "I've never had it before," I admitted. "Had never even heard of it until now."

"No?" Rook asked with a raised brow, taking interest in my comment.

"No," I answered. "There's a lot I don't know about this realm."

"Why is that?" he asked, taking a bite of his bread and leaning in. "You are a daughter of Strong Haven."

Now that was the question of the hour. "I was attacked by a group of fae when I was little, and my mom and dad decided it was safer to distance me away from Faevenly in order to protect me. That's why I don't know much."

Rook narrowed his stare a bit. "That explains many things." He turned his attention to Lady Sonia. "Did you know of this attack on Queen Gabriela?"

"Please, call me Gabriela," I interjected, not wanting the burden of such a title placed on me. At least, not yet. And maybe, not ever.

With a nod from Rook, and even Lady Sonia, she began answering his question. "Yes, I knew of the attack," she answered. "As did Lord Leto. No others were told."

A sarcastic huff escaped my lips. "Especially not me. Not until recently."

The fire crackled, sending tiny bursts of fire floating into the air. I was watching the embers flying away when Rook asked, "What would you like to know, Princess?"

My attention leapt from the fire to him. "What would I like to know?"

"Yes," he said with a slow nod. "You are the head of Strong Haven now, and the future queen of Faevenly. You should know everything about this realm and your fae ancestors."

Stunned, I swallowed the bread I'd been chewing with a large gulp and glanced at Lady Sonia and Uncle Manny.

"Lord Rook is right," Lady Sonia said. "You should know everything about your fae family and your land."

"It makes sense," Uncle Manny said reluctantly, as if he wanted to shield me from painful truths but couldn't anymore. "You should know who you are, *mija*."

"Is it bad?" I asked him, eyeing him before glancing at the others. ""I feel like everything about my fae side is... bad."

"Well," Manny said with a shrug, "it's fae."

Fae... The word was synonymous with beauty and mystery. But I was beginning to understand how fae were also cunning and dangerous.

"Do you know much about my fae side, Uncle Manny?" I asked.

He rubbed his face. "I know the stuff your dad, your mom, and I went through when we were here all those years ago. Though I'm sure there's a lot more I don't know about."

My hunger vanished, replaced by a knot in my gut. I had wanted to know about my mom and her fae family, but life and obligations had gotten in the way. Now, with my future and all of Faevenly at risk, I needed to know everything I could.

"Okay," I said, folding up what was left of my bread and setting it aside. "What do I want to know?" I cleared my throat as I shuffled my thoughts around in my head. "How about everything?"

"Everything," Rook repeated. He raised a brow at

Lady Sonia. "I think you are the best one to tackle that request."

Lady Sonia smoothed out the skirt of her dress, then put away her bread like I had. She angled her body toward me.

"I have been a palace healer to Strong Haven for centuries. I served High King Rowan Strong and High Queen Anise Strong, and before them, High King Rowan's begetters, High King Finial and High Queen Astria."

"Rowan and Anise," I said. "Those were my mom's parents. Or... her begetters. So, my grandparents."

"Yes and no. High King Rowan and High Queen Anise are the begetters of your mother's sister, Lady Malena. But they are not the begetters of your mother. Or, to be more precise, not both of them."

I blinked, her words floating around in my head a few minutes before I asked, "Huh? I don't know what you mean."

"Lady Gabriela," she said slowly and clearly. "Your mother, Lady Celyse, was born unto High King Rowan and a young lady from the human realm."

Her words lingered in the air for a few seconds, like a bad memory or a terrifying dream, before shocking me straight through to my core. I sucked in my breath and held it so tight my chest hurt. "My mom had a human mother? She was... half human?" I turned to my uncle. "Did you know?"

"I did, *mija*. Your mom and dad never wanted to tell you about your grandmother because she was"—his voice trailed off and his throat bobbed from a hard swallow—"executed after your mom was born."

The word echoed in my head and my gut tightened, as if I'd been sucker punched. *Executed?* Before I could make any sort of response, Uncle Manny held up his hand to stop me so he could go on.

"Let me finish the whole story." He wiped his hands on his pants. "High Queen Anise had a child, your mother's sister Malena, the same day a human woman had your mother. The High Queen wanted to execute both the human woman and your mother, but the High King would not let her. So your mother was spared and they let everyone believe the High Queen had birthed twins."

My mind struggled to make sense of it. "But fae can't lie."

"Fae do not have to lie," Lady Sonia explained. "A twist on words can alter the meaning of an entire sentence. Or, in this case, an omission of words. The young lady who carried your mother was hidden away. When your mother was born, and after the young lady was dealt with, the palace presented your mom and Malena together as heirs to the throne. Two healthy princesses. Since Celyse and Malena were indeed sired by the king, it was a true statement, albeit an incomplete statement. The presentation was believed by all."

My mouth had fallen open and I closed it with a soft swallow. "Did my mother know?"

"She found out because I told her," Rook said, with a somewhat softer tone than his usual deep and gruff one. "It was necessary for her to know of her parentage so that she could find out the truth of what the High King and High Queen were doing."

"Truth? What do you mean?" I asked.

"The High King and High Queen were stealing humans and using them as slaves to mine aquoise in the Sublands," he gritted out with anger and pain. "I was on a mission to kill the High Queen to stop their heinous acts because she was responsible. She and Draven, that is. The High King was merely her controlled puppet. Your mother joined my cause when she learned the truth. And your father helped her."

I felt frozen, rooted in place. Lost in a strange feeling of pure and utter betrayal, I had no idea what to say.

Uncle Manny rubbed my arm. "I know it's a lot, *mija*. I'm so sorry. But none of this changes anything about your mom and dad."

"How can you say that, Uncle Manny?" I pinched the bridge of my nose and stayed like that while everything sank in. "Everything I thought I knew about myself is a lie. My mother was half human and never told me. My Strong ancestors were monsters." I pinched even harder, wanting to feel the pain. "No wonder everyone wants to kill the Strongs. We're the bad guys. And liars."

Manny snapped. "*¡Deja eso!*"

His words stung like a slap and left me speechless. He had never yelled at me before.

"I will not allow you to talk about your mother and

her name like that! Or your father! Understand?" He held me in a hard stare before softening his face a bit. "Your mother and father have done everything to protect you, Gabriela. Everything." He looked away and I thought I saw his eyes water. "You will never know the sacrifices they made."

I shrank back, feeling so small and so ungrateful, realizing he was right. My mom and dad had always put me first. Now she was dead, and my dad was with her. I shouldn't blame them for things that were out of their control. My mom had no hand in her parentage or her upbringing.

Hot tears stung my eyes. "I'm sorry, Uncle Manny."

He hugged me and held on tight. "I am too, *mija.*"

We held each other for a long while. When we parted, the mood around the fire stayed somber and no one spoke. It was as if no one wanted to dredge up any more painful memories. As if Uncle Manny and I didn't need any more harsh truths being told. And maybe we didn't. But Rook had one last thing to say.

He rose to his feet and tossed a stick in the fire. "There are many evils in Faevenly. Many untruths. Many hidden agendas." He swung his gaze on me. "But I tell you this with the utmost certainty. The Strongs are the lesser of the evils. And you have the ability to change everything." Whether I was ready or not.

An icy chill raced down my body, and suddenly I felt ice cold despite the roaring fire in front of me.

3

LEAF

Draven had taken me through the shimmer and brought me here, to a dark cave somewhere in Faevenly.

I kept my distance at the back of the small cavity, hands clenched at my sides, and watched as Draven walked back and forth across the cave opening. I had no idea where we were or what we were doing here. Not that it mattered. I was trapped with a mad witch.

And he was plotting something. I could feel it.

His black cloak hung long enough to drag across the craggy ground, but it never did. Instead, it floated a mere hair above the dirt and rock, as if an invisible force kept it from touching the living soil. A force field the sinister soul vamp had conceived and wrapped himself in.

And I had no idea how he did it.

Watching him for a full day now, I never saw him whisper a spell, or flick his hands, or even do anything to his attire. It was as if the power came from his very soul, if he had one, emanating from his pale skin like a thin membrane.

With Draven occupied by his own mind, I got lost

in mine as well, dwelling on how I had gotten myself into my predicament, reliving every regrettable moment that led me here.

With years of pent-up resentment and loathing for Draven building inside of me after all the wicked deeds he had committed over countless years, I had decided to end him. For good. My plan had been to stealth my way into the Strong Haven dungeon and rip his head right off his body.

But he was ready. He was waiting. And I had no idea. I never stood a chance.

It was a cool, brisk day when I visited Strong Haven palace. I spent time with Leto, catching up and exchanging pleasantries. But we did not visit long because he had palace business to attend to, and I had my own agenda.

Knowing the inner workings of the dungeon because I had served as guard there before, I slipped the key away from the entrance where it hung, then secretly made my descent into the dark stairwell undetected.

Winding my way with slow and quiet steps, I found myself plunged in darkness on the bottom floor. My eyes quickly adjusted to my surroundings, spotting a narrow beam of gray light that came from a small opening carved out of the towering ceiling. The haze was enough for me to see the dreadful witch clearly.

Draven lay on a slab stone in the middle of a barred room. Fully dressed, eyes closed, arms resting at his sides. Potion-laden threads, fashioned by Lady

Sonia to subdue him and keep him in a state of sleep, wrapped around his wrists. I remembered those threads well, as they were used on Draven when we captured him all those years ago in the Great Hall, a feat we would not have been able to accomplish without the human witch, Julio.

With a sharp eye on Draven's pale and unmoving face, I eased the key into the lock of his cage. I turned it so slowly it made no sound. With a soft exhale, I eased open the bars and crept in. And when I swooped in to wrap my hands around his neck, he slammed his hands around my arms and compelled me with a single word.

That was all it took for him to control me.

I shoved the memory away, not wanting to think anymore about that day because it made me sick. Like a rod driven deep into my gut. I had freed Draven, the soul-sucking vamp. Now he owned me. Because of him, I had caused the deaths of so many, including Celyse and Julio. I had even given Draven the last remaining piece of aquoise, betraying my friends and the woman who had my heart in the worst possible way.

Would Gabriela ever forgive me? I wouldn't.

I replayed the look of surprise on her face when I took the stone. Recalled her desperately trying to talk me out of my actions, and then later fighting me with her weapon. I was sure she hated me, and with good cause. I was the enemy now. If I survived all this, I would never forgive myself.

A swish of Draven's robe pulled me from my thoughts as he turned to face me. His menacing crystal-white eyes bored into mine, and he clicked his tongue. Like I was nothing more than an inconvenience.

"I have thought of what to do with you," he announced.

He'd been thinking about me this entire time? My gut dropped, but I would not let him know my fear. Instead, I worked my jaw and clenched my hands even tighter, letting my anger seep through me.

"What is that?" I asked through gritted teeth.

He advanced a step. "I am going to bind you to me."

I had no idea what he meant by that, but did not need to know. Any binding to Draven the Witch was a death sentence. My body tensed, and my eyes flicked about, searching for a weapon. Of course, there were none.

He kept his deadly stare on me as he advanced another step. "No weapons. But even if there was one, you would not be able to get it. Not while you are under my compulsion."

He was right. I was utterly powerless. I widened my stance, ready to take whatever he was about to do me. "Why do you need to bind yourself to me if you control me so completely?"

He moved in closer. "For assurances." Like I wasn't already his.

With narrowed eyes, I sneered. "You may do what

you will. But I promise I will kill you at the end of all this."

Draven lifted the corner of his mouth in a sinister smile. "I expect no less from you, Leaf Kane, murderer of your half brother, Alexander Kane. Betrayer of Strong Haven."

Being called a murderer did not bother me, but a betrayer? I pounced at the witch, but he sidestepped me with a whoosh and a flap of his cloak, then slammed his hand around my throat.

"**Stop**," he commanded. "**Stay still**."

His deep voice vibrated in that low octave I knew all too well. The one that worked its way inside me, locking into every part of my body, forcing me to obey no matter how hard I fought his command. My body went slack and I stood motionless. Like a defenseless animal.

Draven studied me with menacing eyes, then cupped his hand around my chin and dug his fingers into my skin. "**Open your mouth**."

A cold rush of fear ripped down my spine as my mouth pried open on its own. Draven licked his lips, then brought his mouth so close to mine our lips nearly met. He drew in a deep breath, and I felt my own breath trickling out of me. My air came out slowly at first, in short bursts, then quickly started whipping out of me like a gust of wind as he slammed his lips on mine. My throat tightened, my chest constricted, and sheer terror descended on me.

Draven was taking my soul. I felt it leaving me.

I knew what it meant for a soul vamp to feed. I had never seen it happen—but I had seen the aftermath—the shriveled corpses that had been sucked dry. And now it was my time to be reduced to nothing but withered remains.

As my breath emptied and my body neared its end, Draven stopped. He dropped his hand and stepped away from me, wiping his mouth. "You may move now."

I crashed to the ground, gasping for air, clutching my chest that burned from the trauma. He glared at me with hate and loathing. "Now part of your essence, your soul, is with me. I own you, Leaf. In all things. Do not forget it."

He spun on his heels, flapped his cloak, and strode out of the cave. When he disappeared from sight, I hunched over and struggled for air. With each gulp that entered my body, my ragged breathing steadied. And when my lung functioning returned to normal, the full implication of what he had done dawned on me.

A part of my soul was now inside of him. He had ruined me. There was no undoing it. I would never be whole again.

I was easing myself up to my feet, watching the cave opening, when something else dawned on me. I was finally alone. Could I simply walk out of the cavern? Knowing Draven, I did not think so, but I had to try.

Taking slow and deliberate steps, I made my way

across the dirt floor. When my boots met the spot where the cave was no more, my body stopped, as if meeting a wall I could not see. I backed up and tried again, this time picking up my pace. But again, the invisible barrier blocked my exit.

I had not expected anything different.

Giving up, I lowered myself onto a boulder. I ran my hands down my trousers and clutched my knees, steadying myself. Draven may have bound himself to me by taking part of my soul, but it did not matter. I would kill the mad witch — blood answering blood; soul against soul.

My life be damned. I would end him.

4

GABRIELA

Lying under the stars on a pallet made of blankets, I stared at the darkest sky with the most brilliant stars I had ever seen. They scattered across the wide-open heavens, like tiny little disco balls, sparkling like a spectacular nighttime show. The view took my breath away—just like Faevenly. The night sky, the day sky, the flowers, the trees... everything here was so vibrant and rich, it almost looked unreal. Like a painting. Or an animated movie.

But just as everything here was beautiful, it was equally deadly. And being here left me feeling anxious and uneasy as my mind replayed everything I had learned about my mom and the Strong side of my family. But Rook's words about the Strongs being the lesser of the evils replayed the loudest, leaving me with a stark realization.

We are all villains. That was the truth no one wanted to say.

I pushed the descriptor out of my brain, refusing to be a villain. I wanted to be good and on the side of right and justice. Yet the longer I thought about everything, the more I knew it wasn't possible.

Sometimes who we are is predetermined, and there's nothing we can do about it.

Glancing over, I checked on Uncle Manny. He was lying on his side on a pallet next to mine, his hands tucked under his head, his mouth open as he slept. Taking a closer look, I saw the movement of his eyes under his eyelids. He was dreaming, and I wondered what about. I hoped that whatever it was, it was nice and not something awful. Especially since I was only beginning to understand the horrors of what he'd been through his first time in Faevenly.

With sleep escaping me, I propped myself up on my forearms and looked around. The roaring fires had dwindled to smaller ones, casting an orange glow about the camp, and everyone was lying down and sleeping. Except for the guards. They were stationed around the perimeter. Among them, I spotted Rook. He was talking to one of the guards with his arms crossed and brow furrowed. I thought of going over to ask if something was wrong, but he caught my stare. He bowed his head in acknowledgment, then folded his arms in front of himself and turned so that his back faced me. Like he didn't want me involved.

"Hmm," I muttered, not liking the way he turned away. If something needed my attention, he would tell me. I hoped. So I eased myself back on my pallet and resumed staring at the skies.

With the soft breeze flowing over me, my thoughts drifted to my mom and dad. The moment I learned about my mom, I knew I needed to see her and ask her the truth about who she was. But I'd been waiting to be alone at night. And also waiting so I could think of the right words to say. Not that there were any right words to ask why she and my dad had kept so much from me my entire life.

I drew in a deep breath, then pulled my soft wool blanket over my head. Under my makeshift cocoon, I closed my eyes and pictured the Passing Place. I visualized the rich green meadow, the bright lavender flowers, the endless blue sky, the apple trees, and the creek where I had seen my mom fishing. I willed myself to go there, my heart aching so fiercely for my mom and dad that a flood of tears clogged my throat.

"I need y'all," I whispered, as tears seeped from the corners of my eyes. "So badly." It came out like a plea.

A drifting feeling overcame me, like the gentle rocking of an ocean. When it stopped, I opened my eyes and found myself on a bed of grass under a bright clear day. I sat up and recognized the same lush lavender meadow where I had met my father. But this time, he was nowhere to be seen.

I climbed to my feet and turned in a small circle, scanning my surroundings. "Dad? Mom?"

I stayed still, waiting for my dad to show himself, when a magnificent white horse appeared at the far end of the meadow. It trotted regally, raising its hooves up high with each step. It wore a gold harness and pulled a flatbed trailer. When it crossed in front of me, I saw three bodies covered in white sheets. I wondered who they were, praying it wasn't Leto or any of the people of Strong Haven as I slowly moved my hand from my forehead, down to my chest, and then from one shoulder across to the other.

"What strange gesture is that?" a small voice asked.

I spun around and saw a boy. He was small and thin, with short blond hair and pointed ears that stuck out sharply. His body had a translucent hue, so I knew he wasn't alive.

"It's the sign of the cross," I explained. "It's something you do when you pray."

He tilted his head for a moment, keeping his inquisitive eyes on me. "I do not understand what you mean."

"It's something from my world," I said. "The human realm."

His brow furrowed, and I could tell he still didn't understand. But I didn't feel like explaining. I knelt down to his eye level. "Why are you here in the Passing Place instead of, you know, passing over?"

He blinked a bit, looked about, then said, "I am waiting to see if my mother and father will join me."

"Oh," I said. "Are they here but somewhere else? Or are they still in Faevenly?"

"I am not sure." He scratched his head. "I thought they were here with me, but I do not remember so well."

Even though he spoke matter-of-factly, a sharp pang of sadness struck me. For him *and* for me, because we were here for the same reason. Waiting for people who might never come. "I'm here looking for my mother and my father too."

"I have not seen a mother nor a father. You are the only person I have seen today." He looked up at the vast blue sky. "I think I mean today. I do not know how long I have been here."

"Yeah," I said, following his line of sight. "I guess it's hard to know things here."

"It is," he said with a shrug. He brought his attention back to me. "What is your name? If I see them, I can tell them you are here."

"My name is Gabriela. What is your name, in case I see your parents?"

"I am Filly."

"Filly—that's a nice name," I said with a smile. "Is that a nickname or your real name?"

"A what?" he asked with a scrunched-up face.

"Um, never mind," I said. "It's nothing."

"You talk in a strange manner, Gabriela," he said.

"I know. I'm sorry. We talk a little differently in the human realm." Before I could say anything else confusing, I said a quick goodbye. "Well, I hope you find your parents, Filly."

"I hope you do too, Gabriela."

He turned and walked in the direction the horse had come from. I stayed there a bit longer before heading to the creek where I had last seen my parents. I made my way across the meadow, over the thick hedge, past the apple trees, and to the babbling flow of water. But it too was empty. I lowered myself onto the bright green grass, feeling sorry for myself, thinking they had passed on and didn't tell me, but I quickly pushed that thought away.

My dad wouldn't have done that to me. No way.

With the breeze blowing and the creek trickling, I started getting sleepy. One yawn led to another, and I decided to lay down on the grass and rest. The second my head hit the ground, a hand shook my shoulder.

"Gabriela?"

My eyes fluttered open to see Uncle Manny hovering over me. "*Mija*, I let you sleep in as long as I could, but we're packing up to leave now."

"What?" A soft pink hue stretched across the morning sky as birds sang and flitted about. Everyone bustled around the camp, gathering pallets and loading things into bags. I sat up and rubbed my eyes. "It feels like I just went to bed."

"You were out," he said, patting my leg. "You can sleep in the carriage if you need more rest."

"Yeah," I said with a groan. "I think I will."

After our carriages were loaded up and everyone had boarded, we took off at an easy trot that slowly increased to a steady pace. I had wanted to nap, but with the bright sky and the jostling ride, I couldn't. With my arms crossed, I turned my body away from Uncle Manny and Lady Sonia and stared out the window, wondering where my parents had been.

But on the other side of the carriage, it was anything but quiet. Uncle Manny couldn't stand the silence, and he chatted with Lady Sonia about anything and everything. He asked about the weather, the road, the carriage, our bags, and our next meal. He voiced concern about my mom and dad, and expressed anger over Leaf. In between, he told jokes and made Lady Sonia laugh. Every now and again, I'd chuckle too. He was all over the place with his emotions and his train of thought. Not that I could blame him.

On the third day, the landscape began to change. It was so gradual, I didn't notice at first. The thick, rich green fields, shrubs, and trees had thinned out, giving way to rocky and dusty terrain. The air changed too, and became much drier with little to no humidity.

"We are entering the Sublands now," Lady Sonia announced.

Uncle Manny peeked out the window. "Yep. We sure are."

"This is the Sublands?" I sat up and leaned against the side of the carriage so I could see ahead of us. With the day growing brighter, I spotted pinnacles and spires of earthen tones like purple, yellow, tan, and gray. Some of them were tall and thin; others were big and wide.

"It's pretty amazing, isn't it?" asked Uncle Manny.

"It really is," I muttered. "Like a geologist's wonderland."

"A wonderland indeed," Lady Sonia said. "But the Sublands have been anything but highly regarded. Centuries ago, the Strongs deemed the area uninhabitable. So they carved out the rocky parcel, separating the land from the other provinces. They sent outcasts and renegades here as punishment, and let the area fend for itself. Since humans were regarded as lesser beings, many of them that crossed into this realm—those that were not executed—ended up here."

I swallowed as I rubbed my neck. "But it's not like that anymore, right?"

"It is not." Sonia kept her eye on the landscape. "Things changed when the Caileans rose to power."

"The Caileans?"

Lady Sonia nodded. "Yes, the Caileans. They are the fae family that were put in charge of the Sublands. They took in Rook, and later Leaf. They were responsible for turning this region around when they began mining precious rocks and minerals. They are the ones that discovered aquoise. But then the Strongs swept in and took ownership of their operation and the land, using the Caileans as grunt workers and overseers."

My gaze drifted back outside, to the rocky landscape that erupted from the ground. "With the aquoise gone, what has become of the area?"

"Well," Uncle Manny cut in. "We kinda blew up the main city."

I swung my stare on him. "Y'all did what?" I blinked, sure I'd misheard him.

He ran his fingers through his thick dark hair. "Your mom, dad, Leaf, Leto, Rook, and I, and a fae named Jaid, blew up a cavern where an aquoise pool was and the whole city kinda came crashing down."

I sat stunned. "But why? Especially if that rock was so precious?"

"Because it was Draven's source of energy. So we had to destroy it. We had no other choice," he explained.

"Wow," I muttered, my mind processing everything. "Did anyone get hurt?"

Uncle Manny nodded. "We lost Jaid, your mom's childhood best friend. There were also many in the Sublands main city that died."

"Jeez," I whispered. "I bet the Caileans were pretty angry about that."

"The Caileans were executed by Draven," Manny said in a low voice. "Draven even executed your mom's dad, right in front of us, with Alexander Kane by his side."

I shuddered as tingles of fear raced down my body. I knew Draven was evil, someone to be feared. But he executed the Caileans, and my grandfather? That put him on another level of evil. Right there with the Kanes.

The carriage took a hard dip, sending us sliding from one side of our seats to the other. It righted itself with a jerk and then stopped. I shifted back to where I was sitting and peered out the window.

"We've stopped again?" I asked. My pulse quickened.

Lady Sonia frowned. "It seems we have."

My hand went to the back of my neck, waiting for a warning tingle to strike, but nothing happened.

"Are you getting a witchy vibe?" Uncle Manny asked.

"No, I'm not. Not yet anyway."

"Well, that's good." He grabbed the handle to the door. "Let's go see what's going on, then."

We exited the carriage and started for the front of our caravan where Rook was when two fae on tall, magnificent horses came into view—a man and a woman. They wore copper-colored pants and long-sleeved shirts, the same color as the rock all around us. Their horses were copper-colored too, with rich red manes. Behind them and farther back were five others on horses.

"That doesn't look good," Uncle Manny muttered.

"It does not," Lady Sonia agreed.

As we neared, I saw that they had piercing blue eyes and wore their long dark hair in thick braids. I also realized the woman wasn't really a woman after all, but a girl about my age. Same with the guy—he was young too. But then I did a double take, realizing the girl held me in a death glare. I swallowed, trying not to let her unnerve me, and lifted my chin a little higher.

"Daughter of Strong Haven," the intimidating girl said slowly, articulating each letter with vicious loathing, and suddenly I really and truly understood the meaning of the phrase *if looks could kill*.

I flashed a raised brow to Uncle Manny, and he returned the look, letting me know he had no idea what was up with that girl. He also moved in closer to me.

Rook answered with formal introductions. "Lady

Verona and Lord Adrius of the Sublands, this is Princess Gabriela of Strong Haven, Manny Vela of the human realm, and Lady Sonia, Strong Haven healer."

Lady Sonia lowered her head, and Uncle Manny and I followed. "I am pleased to make your acquaintance," Sonia said.

"I as well," I said, matching Sonia's tone and formality, realizing I needed to act every part the princess.

Lord Adrius's horse stamped, and he tugged on the reins. He kept his attention on Rook. "We are here to inform you that the council has received word of Draven the Witch's escape, Strong Haven's abandonment, and the gathering of the other provinces against Strong Haven. We have also received word that you, Lord Rook, have offered safe haven to the Strong people. However, said offer was not approved by the Sublands council and as such cannot be honored."

What? Surprise slammed into me. I shot my uncle Manny a look.

"Whoa, whoa, whoa," he said to the guy, mirroring my emotions and stepping forward. "What are you saying exactly?" He turned to Rook. "What the hell is he saying?"

Lady Verona glared at Uncle Manny. "Lord Adrius is saying you must turn away at once, human. Your party and your people are not welcome in the Sublands."

Rook's nostrils flared. "You speak to him, you speak to me, Verona!"

"Then I speak to you," she said in a low, warning tone.

Rook clenched his hands at his sides and stepped closer to the horses. "You would turn away the helpless and defenseless? You would treat them the way our people have been treated for centuries? Does being a Sublander mean nothing to you? We are better than that!"

"It means everything to me, Rook! Everything to us!" Verona spat out. "Our city was destroyed because of the Strongs! We will not lose what we have rebuilt because of them!"

Adrius slid off his horse. He shot Verona a warning glare, then placed his hand on Rook's shoulder. "It is done, Lord Rook. The council has voted. Even without you, the majority has spoken. The Sublands must protect itself." He glanced at me. "The Strongs are on their own." The words hit harder than any blow.

Rook brushed Adrius's hand off his shoulder. He backed away from the fae with fire in his eyes, and stood next to me. "They are not alone."

"Fool," the girl hissed.

"Fool, Verona?" Rook asked. "You are calling me a fool?"

Verona didn't back down. "Yes. I am." Her horse matched her agitated mood and twirled in a circle. "You would risk your life and others for the Strongs when they have committed atrocities against so many and decimated our city and our keep." She glared at me. "Her name is not worth it."

"Enough, Verona!" Rook called out.

"Yes, Verona," Adrius said, glowering. "Leave it." He got back on his horse. "The Sublands has voted. The matter has been decided and the message has been delivered. Rook will do what he will. Let us depart now."

Verona nodded at Adrius, then directed her gaze at Rook. I thought I detected a hint of sadness in her eyes. "We wish you well, Lord Rook."

My gut sank at the finality in his voice, not for me or Uncle Manny or Rook or Lady Sonia, but for all the maid servants and ladies in the carriages who were being abandoned. They didn't deserve to suffer because of something that happened to the Sublands so long ago.

They pulled their horses' reins and started turning. Holding on to that glimmer of sympathy from Verona, I stepped into my courage as a princess of Strong Haven and called out, "Wait!" The word came out sharper than I expected.

The pair circled their horses around and faced us. Verona looked annoyed. Adrius looked concerned. "Yes, my lady?" he asked.

I motioned to the carriages. "This caravan is the first wave to leave Strong Haven and consists of ladies and maid servants. If the Sublands would at least take them, it would be most appreciated."

"Yes," Rook added. "Please, give these people refuge. They have done nothing wrong."

The girl frowned, but before she could say anything, Adrius spoke. "We will take them."

"Adrius, no," she hissed.

"I will take responsibility," he shot back.

She pulled her horse away and stared off into the distance while Adrius hopped off his horse and started making arrangements with Rook.

Uncle Manny moved close to me and whispered. "What is her problem?"

"Well, we're the villains. Remember?"

He studied me with raised brows, then lowered them slowly. "I guess we are."

Maid Gidna rushed over to me. "My lady, my dear. I am without words right now!" Tears glistened in her eyes as she clutched the top of her shirt. "I heard the exchange from my carriage and cannot believe this is happening!"

"It's okay, Gidna. We'll figure something out," I said with a calm voice, while inside I had no idea if that was true.

Rook waved me over to him, and together we went to each carriage and told the drivers and the passengers they were being escorted to the Sublands by Lord Adrius and Lady Verona and that Lord Rook, Lady Sonia, Manny, and I were heading west. I kept my voice sure, trying to act like the leader I was supposed to be, as if I knew what I was doing and everything was fine.

Little did they know how lost I felt, and how everything was anything but fine.

With that task completed, Rook had four guards

give us their horses while they piled into the carriage Lady Sonia, Uncle Manny, and I had been in.

The last thing I had to do was the hardest—say goodbye to Gidna. She wrapped her arms around my waist while I bent down and wrapped mine around her shoulders.

"You are a good girl, Gabriela. With so many wonderful gifts from your father's side of the family and also your mother's side. Do not ever forget that." She pulled away and cupped my face with her thick, rough hands. "Your gifts will serve you well. I know it."

I swallowed, forcing my tears to stay down and putting on a brave face. "Thank you, Gidna."

She smiled, then released my face and stepped away. "I will see you soon, my dear." I hoped she was right.

I nodded and smiled back. "Yes. Soon."

Uncle Manny wrapped his arm around me and together we watched Maid Gidna get in the carriage. With a wave and a shout from Lord Adrius, the Sublanders led the caravan away, leaving a cloud of red dirt in their wake.

A huge sigh escaped me. "Do you think they'll be okay?" I asked Uncle Manny softly, worried they wouldn't be treated right in the Sublands.

"Of course they will," Rook answered quickly. I turned around, not even realizing he was standing behind me and Uncle Manny. "The Sublanders will do their duty," he assured. "Lord Adrius will see to it. As will Lady Verona."

Uncle Manny pointed in the direction of the caravan. "*That* Lady Verona? The one that hates the Strongs? And seems to hate you too?"

"She does not hate me." He picked up our bags and started hooking them to the saddles of our horses. "She and Adrius were but small children when the Sublands main city was destroyed. They are all that survived from their family. They lived alone as orphans, struggling to stay alive. I became aware of their plight and helped raise them."

"Damn," Uncle Manny said in a low voice. "I'm sorry, Rook."

"Do not be. It was long ago. The people of the Sublands do not want nor need pity."

I watched the caravan fade from view, feeling awful about yet another horrible thing that had happened because of my fae family. "Needed or not needed, I'm sorry too."

"Guard your feelings, my lady," Rook warned. He stopped what he was doing and narrowed his stare on me. "Feelings get people killed."

He didn't have to say Leaf's name for me to know what he meant. I had strong feelings for Leaf and had shared so much with him—my emotions, my heart, my body, my everything. Now he was with Draven, and Draven was going to use Leaf against me in any way he could.

Was I ready for that?

"Do you understand, Gabriela?" he asked. "Protect yourself above all others."

"Yes, I understand," I said, not liking all the pressure on me, but understanding it. I was a Strong. The only Strong, now that my mother was gone. And I needed to act like it.

"She gets it, Rook," Uncle Manny added in my defense.

Rook finished securing our bags on the horses, then started checking their bridles. Considering the massive stature of the horses, I thought it'd be easier for me to ride in jeans instead of a long dress.

"Before we go, I'd like to change my clothes real quick."

Uncle Manny glanced at my long dress. "I actually think that's a good idea." He unstrapped my bag and handed it to me. He considered Lady's Sonia's equally long dress in the process. "Would you like to change clothes too?"

"I am accustomed to riding in this attire. Thank you, Manny."

Crouching down, I opened my bag and pulled out my faded jeans and my long-sleeved purple shirt. Seeing that the others had moved away and turned their backs to me, I quickly undressed and put on my regular clothes in a flash.

"I'm finished. Y'all can turn around now."

I folded my dress and shoved it in my bag, remembering how, not long ago, I was a regular, jean-wearing girl worried about a dumb calculus test. Now, I was the last standing Strong family member, turned away by an entire people.

I couldn't feel any smaller.

"I'll take that," Uncle Manny said, pulling me away from my thoughts and taking my bag. He secured it in place, then helped me climb atop my horse. Once I was on, it was Uncle Manny's turn to get on his, but he didn't look too excited.

"What is it, Uncle Manny?" I asked.

A nervous laugh escaped his lips. "The last time I rode a horse was here in Faevenly." He swallowed. "It wasn't a great experience."

I had ridden a horse years ago at summer camp and loved it. But looking at Uncle Manny's furrowed brow and his tan skin that looked nearly pale, I could tell he hated it. Maybe he was even terrified of it.

"But *mija*," he added quickly, "I'll be fine. I'm just an old dude with achy bones. That's all."

"You're only in your forties, Uncle Manny. You're not old," I laughed.

He shoved his boot in the stirrup, hopped, and swung his leg over his horse. "Tell that to these ageless fae."

Our horses started moving around, stamping their hooves and whinnying in turn.

"I think our rides are ready to go," Lady Sonia said.

"Where are we going, anyway?" I asked. "Rook said west earlier, but where exactly?"

"Strong Haven West," Rook announced. "To the manor there."

Uncle Manny's horse moved in a circle. "What

about Leto and the others?" he asked. "What will happen to them?"

"I asked Lord Adrius to send them word of our new destination. He will do so when they arrive in the city."

My horse began circling like Uncle Manny's, its outbursts growing louder with each movement. "We should get going, then. This guy is ready to bolt."

"Get going slowly," Uncle Manny cautioned with an edgy laugh. "Okay? Not too fast, please."

Rook nodded. "Not too fast."

Rook took off at an easy pace, and the rest of the horses followed. We rode west, the setting sun blazing before us, the wind sharp against our faces. The Sublands had turned us away, and it felt like the last safe place in the world had closed its gates. With each stride, I wondered where my parents were—and whether Leaf was still alive to see the same fading light.

The farther we rode, the more it felt like everything I loved was slipping beyond reach. And there was nothing I could do to stop it.

5

LEAF

The day crept by and Draven did not return. He stayed away through the night. And when the new day dawned and I had come to terms with my predicament, I rose and moved to the cave opening so I could study my surroundings.

"Why here?" I muttered to myself, knowing full well that Draven did everything with purpose. I ran my hands over the rough wall. "Where is here anyway?"

The jagged cave opening was on the smaller side, around ten feet high and ten feet wide. Tall, thin trees and sparse brush shrouded the space just a few steps away, and dirt and leaves covered the ground. I crouched down and narrowed my gaze. Small animal prints tracked through the area as far as the eye could see, resembling rabbit, raccoon, and deer tracks. Birds of all sizes swooped and soared from branch to branch, whistling and cawing.

I wondered what creatures resided in these woods, and if any of them could help me.

Scooping up a handful of dirt, I tossed it with an easy swing. It sailed past my invisible barrier and sprinkled about the ground.

"So, only I am trapped here," I muttered. "Not the elements."

I scooped up another handful of dirt. This time, I packed it tightly in my palm, then hurled it as far as I could. Bits of rock and sand sprinkled onto a bushy area, sending a flutter of leaves and twigs exploding into the sky. I studied the display, realizing I was not observing leaves or twigs at all, but sprites. A colony of wood sprites.

"Sprites! I need help! I am trapped here!" I shouted.

The small creatures spun in a blur and flew up into the air, soaring away and disappearing from sight. But one turned back. It hovered in the air, swaying back and forth for a bit, before zipping over to me with long golden-hued wings.

It twirled, then flitted closer. It stopped short of entering the cave, staying outside the opening and hovering at eye level. It was a lady wood sprite with skin as brown as tree bark and yellow eyes that matched the tufts of yellow moss that started at the top of her head and traveled down her back.

"Hello, lovely fae," she said in a high-pitched voice. "Are you injured?"

"Hello, beautiful wood sprite," I replied, with a smile and a bow of my head. "I am injured, but healing well." I avoided touching the cuts and bruises on my face. "I am Leaf of the Sublands."

She bowed low. "I am Majestic, of these trees."

Gazing about, I asked, "Where are these trees?"

She blinked, then twirled. "You do not know where you are standing?"

"No," I shook my head. "I do not. I was taken, and now I am imprisoned here."

She gasped and pressed her tiny branch-like fingers to her mouth. She held them there a few moments before dropping them and asking, "Imprisoned by whom?"

I did not think I should mention Draven's name, so simply said, "An evil being."

"Oh my, oh my. I have not seen an evil being in these parts." She spun around, her eyes scanning the woods. "I do not see one now either."

"We only arrived yesterday, and my captor has left me here. But I am unable to walk out of this cave."

"Oh my, oh my." She peered at the cave opening, searching for whatever was holding me in place. "I do not see any impediment to your departure."

"My impediment is invisible. Nothing can be done for it." Not by me.

She zipped in and circled my head. Then she hovered in front of my face. "I am not impeded."

"The barrier is only meant for me."

"Only for the lovely fae," she said, as she batted her long gold eyelashes, her mouth downturned in a frown. "So very sad."

I held out my palm. She landed on my skin with a tickle, her lashes still flashing at me. She was unusual, as I had never seen a sprite with gold wings.

"Majestic is a fitting name for you, dear sprite," I smiled.

A yellow-tinted flush sprinkled her cheeks. She wrapped her hands together in front of her body and turned away. "You are too kind, Lovely Leaf." Then she asked, "Do you still wish to know where you stand?"

"I do, please."

She straightened her back, as if looking proud and pleased to provide me with answers. "You are in a wooded area to the far south of Strong Haven."

"I see," I said, wondering why Draven would be here of all places. There had to be a reason. "Thank you for letting me know."

As I studied her more closely, an idea began to form. Perhaps she could be my voice and deliver a message to Gabriela and the others and let them know I was all right. And more importantly, that my wrong-doings were not my own. Perhaps, with that knowl-edge, Gabriela might begin to forgive me. It was the only hope I had left.

"Majestic, if you will allow it, may I ask a favor of you?"

She batted her eyelashes. "I will allow it."

"Dear sprite, I would be most grateful if you would—"

Before I could form another word, she let out a sharp gasp and zoomed away like a bolt of lightning. A soft shimmery glow materialized in front of me. Small at first, it stretched out long and wide, revealing my villainous captor, dressed in all black. He didn't step through, but instead beckoned me to him.

"**Come**," he commanded in his smooth and sinister voice.

His words pushed me forward, forcing me to move step by step until I crossed through the shimmer. When I was all the way through, he collapsed it with a swoop and tucked it away in his cloak.

We were standing before Strong Haven Palace. The four-story gold-and-ivory structure sparkled under the sun. Rows of rectangular windows lined the facade, and magnificent gold spires dotted the roof. Pavement made of gravel and brick spanned the front of the palace, creating a circular road. Glancing down, I saw evidence of horse hooves and carriage wheels driving away from the palace, traveling to the main road. My gaze swept back up to the structure, looking for hints of life, but found none.

"Where have they gone?" I asked.

The witch ignored me and made his way to the ornately carved wooden double door. When we neared, a doorman swung it open. He was small and slender with a delicate face, short-cropped brown hair, big brown eyes, and freckles. He wore dark pants and a dark shirt with an olive-colored vest. He swallowed when he saw us and quickly bowed his head.

I had spent a lot of time at Strong Haven Palace and did not recognize the poor young doorman, but I recognized pure fright when I saw it. Draven must have brought him here, as well as the other servants I could not see but could hear shuffling in the distance.

"M-m-master Draven, I was not expecting you b-b-back so soon," he stuttered with his eyes cast down.

Draven ignored him and continued walking as if the doorman was not even there and had not even spoken. I flashed the young servant a look of warning, then waved him away. He scuttled back, closed the door, and held his tongue.

We made our way through the foyer and down a hallway dimly lit by floating orbs. A few servants emerged from various room as we passed, and they gaped at us with looks of terror. Most of them tiptoed away. One dropped a vase of sunflowers. But Draven paid them no heed.

Again, I did not recognize a single face. I wondered where the witch had gotten these servants. Poor creatures. They were probably compelled, like me. I also wondered where everyone in the palace had gone.

He glided by with a sinister cadence. With me trailing him, I was sure everyone who saw us thought the worst of me too. And they would have been right. Draven owned me. In every way that mattered. I was capable of the same atrocities as him now.

Turning down another corridor, we came upon a small door. A door I knew all too well. It was plain and crude, fashioned with the thickest wood. It led to the deep dungeon.

Draven stopped in front of it. With a fingertip touch, he pushed the door open, revealing a dark, winding stairwell. A breath of cold air tinged with damp stone and the metallic scent of rust and age wafted over me.

He beckoned me forward, then followed from behind. Our boots thudded against the stone steps as we descended down the narrow stairwell. When we got to the barred cage at the ground floor, Draven flapped his cloak and spun around to study me. He motioned with his long thin fingers.

"**Enter**."

I focused on my legs, willing them to not obey, but they paid me no heed. With reluctant movement, I strode into the small room Draven had occupied for so many years. I stopped under the narrow light that came in through the small opening high up in the ceiling, then turned around to face him.

"Where are the people of Strong Haven?" I demanded.

His lips curved in a sinister smile. "They fled like the rats they are and set off for the Sublands. But sadly for them, they were turned away."

"Turned away from the Sublands?" I asked, astonished.

"Yes, turned away. Now they head for Strong Haven West." He clicked his tongue in mock pity. "Too bad for them I have a plan to send deadly assassins their way. I am afraid they will perish oh so miserably. With them gone, the Kanes will take their place as high rulers, with me at their side to assist them in whatever way I can."

Rage surged through me. I wanted to lunge, grab him by the throat, and squeeze the life out of him. But my body refused to comply.

"Come now, Leaf. I can feel your feeble attempt to resist me. But I assure you, it is for naught."

I stepped back, realizing he was right, then decided to prod him for more information. "What of the other provinces?"

"They are following my orders and standing down. For the time being, that is, allowing me to take care of their little problem called Gabriela."

"But I am the one who killed Alexander! Not Gabriela!" My voice ricocheted through the stone chamber, raw and ragged against the walls.

He laughed. "It is no matter. She is a daughter of Strong Haven and has always been the target. But never fear, Leaf. Once she is handled, her bloodline will be extinct. After her removal, her allies will suffer gravely. Especially you."

"So you are claiming Strong Haven as your own? And killing everyone in your path?" I asked between clenched teeth.

"Claiming?" He raised a brow. "I do not have to claim anything. This place has been mine for a long time. I simply allowed the Strongs to reside here. It is the greater of all the palaces, after all. It is most grand and affords many amenities—spacious rooms, lush gardens, and, of course, close proximity to Torch Lake. As for killing everyone in my path, they should not have wandered there."

Torch Lake housed the shimmers that floated down from the stratus, and the Strongs were the caretakers. The glowy portals floated along the surface of the water, like opaque bubbles. Interference with them was strictly forbidden in order to prevent fae tampering with the human realm, though many knew the Strongs were the worst violators.

But then something occurred to me. Why would Draven mention the lake?

"Torch Lake?" I asked. "What interest do you have in the lake?"

Draven narrowed his stare. "It is no concern of yours," he snarled. "Not yet, anyway." He flapped his cloak and turned to leave. "You will stay here until I release you."

Draven moved out of the cage, disappearing into the darkness as he walked back up the stairs. With him gone, the air lightened, but my body stayed tense. Assassins were headed for the west, and Gabriela and the others were in trouble. And Draven meant ill with Torch Lake.

I circled the small space, seeing if there was any place where I could get out, but found none. Draven's invisible barrier held strong, and the dungeon itself was built without flaws. With my hopes of escape sinking, and my worry for Gabriela and the others growing, I pounded the stone wall.

"I must get out of here!" There had to be a way. I pounded again and again and again, not caring about the blood trickling from my knuckles or the pain radiating through my hand. The woman who had my heart, and my friends who were with her, were going to die because of me, and there was nothing I could do about it.

With my chest heaving and my body shaking, I lowered myself to the ground. I pulled in my knees and wrapped my arms around my legs, leaning my head down.

"I am so sorry, Gabriela," I whispered. "So very sorry." The words weren't enough.

I pictured her perfectly in my mind. Her flawless sun-kissed skin, long dark hair with silver streaks, brown eyes with flecks of gold and green, full and beautiful lips. She had given herself to me, and I had taken her. And I wished I had not. She deserved so much better than me.

A ruffling wisp took me from my self-pity. It sounded so faint I was not sure if I was hearing anything at all. Raising my head, I eyed the opening at the top of the dungeon and held my breath so I could hear better.

"Leaf?" a small voice asked. "Is that you, Lovely Leaf?"

"Majestic?"

Her tiny body with fluttering golden wings came into view as she flitted down from the opening, flying back and forth until she hovered in front of my face. She smiled, then spotted my bloodied hands and gasped.

"Oh my, oh my. You are injured! Lovely Leaf!"

Ignoring my hands, I asked, "How did you ever find me?"

"When you stepped into the shimmery glow with that evil being, I zoomed in undetected."

I smiled. "You are most brave, little sprite."

She batted her eyelashes. "You honor me with such a compliment, Lovely Leaf. I thank you." She landed on my knee and sat down with her legs tucked under her. "I am ready to hear your request for assistance. If I am able to oblige, I will."

My mind scrambled as I thought of how she could help me when a thought sprang to mind. "My friends are traveling from the Sublands to Strong Haven West, and the evil being has assassins he is sending to slaughter them."

She gasped and placed her tiny hands on her mouth. "Oh my, oh my. That is so very dreadful!"

I brought my face closer to her. "But if you can get to them with a warning, they can flee and hide away. Do you think you can do that?"

She stood with a hop and placed her hands on her hips. "Yes. I can do that."

"Thank you, Majestic. Do you know where the Strong Haven West manor house is?"

She offered me a resolute nod. "I do indeed."

"Good. When you get to the manor house, ask for Gabriela. Tell her Draven has assassins. Tell her she and the others need to leave immediately. Tell her..." There was so much more I wanted to say, but even if Majestic was able to deliver the message, I did not know exactly how to convey the deepest remorse that had shredded my heart into pieces.

"Tell her what, Lovely Leaf?"

My voice lowered as my guilt soared. "Tell her to please be careful."

"I will tell her." Her wings fluttered as she lifted herself from my knee.

"Thank you, Majestic. I will forever be indebted to you for your help." The words felt hollow on my tongue, useless against Draven and his wicked way. But I had to try.

She hovered before me, her wings glimmering faintly in the gloom. Then she drifted close and pressed a tiny kiss to my forehead—a whisper of warmth in the cold. "You are most welcome, Lovely Leaf."

She zipped upward, a streak of gold vanishing through the darkness the way she had come. I watched until even the shimmer of her wings was gone, then bowed my head.

I prayed to the sun, the moon, and every star that might still listen to a wretched being like me that she would reach Gabriela before Draven's assassins did.

It was all I could do.

6

DRAVEN

I emerged from the dark and musty dungeon, eager to set my plan in motion and hungry for the death of the daughter of Strong Haven. Her vile human blood did not belong in Faevenly. Nor did it belong on any throne. And so far, my plan to eradicate her was proceeding smoothly.

I had Leaf under my control. The provinces answered to me. Although the Sublands had taken in the Strong Haven refugees, Gabriela and her band were cast away and now headed west. Little did they know they would face certain death there, and at my hand.

With my cloak drifting behind me, I continued down the corridor past the cookhouse and to the healing chamber. I strode into the herb-laden room and did a quick scan. Shelves lined every inch of wall space, holding vials and jars of different sizes. They contained flowers, herbs, roots, liquids, dirt, and powders. There was even a large jar of the green healing water from the Green Falls, the item I needed most for my precious aquoise.

Eager to see my treasure, and still so pleased with myself at how that fool Leaf had stolen it for me, I approached the wooden table in the middle of the room and examined the large jar of green liquid I had set there earlier. My precious blue stone sparkled at the bottom, like a promise of power. It had been soaking for hours now and had tripled in size, with small spikes of growth jutting out in all directions.

"So beautiful," I murmured.

I needed this last remaining piece of the precious rock so I could grow it. Although I could strengthen myself by consuming souls and I took great pleasure in ending lives, I needed the aquoise for other purposes —like equipping my allies to perform certain tasks for me.

Like ending Gabriela.

There was also my larger plan for the purification of Faevenly.

Taking a long wooden spoon, I scooped out the stone and placed it on a wooden tray. Then I took a pick and a hammer and with a light tap cracked off a small piece. I dropped the bigger chunk back in the jar, then placed the smaller one into a mortar and got busy grinding.

"M-M-Master Draven," a trembling voice said.

I halted my task and turned to see a servant standing just outside the threshold of the door. Small-framed, wide-eyed, and trembling, he gulped when my stare met his. "Lord K-K-Kane and his men are here."

"See them to the receiving room. Then bring the two fastest horses to the front of the palace and wait there for me."

"Yes, Master."

He scurried away while I continued working the granules into a fine powder. When I had them the way I wanted, I took a small cup, poured the powder in, and topped it off with a dash of ground herbs from the shelves—sage, rosemary, and rhodiola rosea.

With the ingredients all together, I emptied the contents into a chalice. I took a bottle of aged wine from the shelf and poured enough to mix in the herbs. I brought it to my nose and inhaled. Finding the aroma perfectly intoxicating, I set out for the receiving room.

Taking my time, I entered the silver-hued room with slow and deliberate steps. The drapes on the floor-to-ceiling windows along the back wall were open, allowing streams of sunlight to pour in. The gleam highlighted the sparkling flecks of gold in the marble floors, showcasing the opulence and wealth of the palace.

Two plush oversized white chairs took up the space in the middle of the room, and between them sat a small gold table. Before the chairs sprawled an ornate rug of gold and silver with an intricate pattern of vines.

My visitors were standing on the floor covering and turned to watch my entrance. Lord Kane, the elder of his house, had streaks of silver running through his long dark hair. Weariness shrouded his eyes, and small thin lines gathered across his forehead. To his right was the younger Kane, a boy barely old enough to wield a sword. He had the same piercing blue eyes as his father and his deceased brother, Alexander, but did not share the same black hair. His was silver. Two guards flanked the duo, bearing daggers at the waist and fighting sticks on their backs.

Holding the simple wooden chalice before me, I kept my intimidating focus ahead as I strode through the room and lowered myself on one of the chairs. I placed my cup on the table, then raised my gaze to Lord Kane.

"Speak."

"Lord Draven," he said with a reverent nod. "Thank you for this audience." He motioned to his heir. "This is Bladen, my youngest son and my heir." He motioned to the men behind him. "These are my most trusted guards." Then he said to them, "This is Draven the Witch."

Though Lord Kane and the guards worked to hide their fear and awe at being in my presence, I saw it still. It lurked in the darkest part of their eyes, like a shadow afraid of the light. But the boy made no attempt to hide his emotions. His eyes were wide and his mouth slightly parted.

Although I knew the purpose of their visit, I spoke with formality and indifference. "You may present your request."

Lord Kane stepped forward. "I demand vengeance for the death of my son," he spat. Anger tightened his jaw and clenched his hands. "I demand the life of Leaf from the Sublands, and I also demand the life of Gabriela, daughter of Strong Haven."

I narrowed my eyes at the desperate fae and said in a slithering tone, "No one makes demands of me, Lord Kane. Not ever. Or perhaps you do not value your life?" My gaze trailed to the young boy. "Or the life of your last remaining heir?"

Lord Kane drew in a steadying breath and shifted his stance. "I do value those things, Lord Draven. I assure you. And I apologize for the lack of decorum with my requests. But my eldest son is dead, my lineage altered forever, and I deserve recompense." He drew in another breath, the tension evident now in his raised shoulders. "I humbly request your assistance in obtaining justice for me and my house, and request the lives of Lord Leaf and Princess Gabriela."

I held him in my gaze, waiting a few long seconds before responding. "Ah, a humble request for justice." I lifted myself up to my feet and steepled my fingers together in front of me. I circled the group, my steps light, my cloak flowing behind me. I knew what his petition would be, and I was ready.

"Leaf of the Sublands is mine." And always would be. I paused my step and cast a sinister glare of warning in his direction, then continued on. "But I am prepared to offer assistance with the daughter of Strong Haven, as I am aligned with your interest in seeking her permanent removal."

Lord Kane hesitated, and his lip twitched. He

wanted Leaf, but he must have wanted his own life more because he tipped his head and said, "That would be most appreciated."

"Very well, then." I halted my circular path and moved back to my seat. "I have received word that the daughter of Strong Haven, Lord Rook, Lady Sonia, and a human are traveling as we speak from the Sublands to the Strong Haven manor in the west. There is no telling how long they will stay there. But if your guards leave now, they can arrive at the same time as Gabriela and her allies and finish them off once and for all."

Lord Kane frowned. "If she is traveling from the Sublands, she will be at least a day, even two, ahead of my men. There is no way they can get there that quickly, especially without stopping along the way."

"Then do not stop." It was that simple.

He balked. "What do you mean? How so? Unless you are referring to calling for the Enbarr, though I doubt they would respond for such a request."

Enbarr only responded to those with pure intentions, and Lord Kane knew that. "I do not mean the Enbarr, Lord Kane. I have speedy horses I can provide for your men. They are conditioned to run twenty-four to seventy-two hours without stopping. Though it should only take closer to twenty-four to get from here to the west with no stops."

Lord Kane huffed. "Though that may be, even the most skilled rider cannot keep a hard pace like that."

"Any rider can maintain that pace—with a little

help." I motioned to the chalice. "This liquid will provide your men with the stamina, endurance, and strength to make the journey with no problem."

He considered the drink. "What is in the liquid?"

My lips curled in delight. "It is a mixture containing elements of aquoise."

The elder Kane's brows shot up. "I thought aquoise no longer existed. That it had all been destroyed."

"Oh, it exists. But only for me." As it should.

"Is that so?" he asked, glancing at his men from the corner of his eye.

"It is so."

Lord Kane cleared his throat, his eyes fixed on the chalice for a few long seconds before saying, "I must have a moment to confer with my guards."

I rose with a swish and stood before the pathetic fae, my glare boring into him. "You misunderstand the rights you have with me," I hissed. My voice dropped to something colder. "Your men will drink from the chalice. They will ride to the Strong Haven West manor. They will take the lives of Gabriela, Lord Rook, Lady Sonia, the human, and anyone else who gets in their way. And they will bring me their heads."

The elder fae kept his stance, refusing to back away from my stare, as if he could challenge me. *Fool.* I stood taller, heat boiling inside me as I prepared to drop my glamour and wipe Lord Kane, his heir, and his men from existence, when he wisely backed down and lowered his eyes.

"As you wish, Lord Draven!"

I kept my steely glare on him as the fire inside of me cooled and my fury subsided. No one dared defy me and lived. But lucky for him, I would not need to kill him today. I flapped my cloak behind me and moved for the chalice.

I raised it up with both hands and extended it toward Lord Kane. "Your guards will drink this mixture."

He waved his guards over to me. One took the chalice and drank half of the liquid, then handed it to the other, who finished it off. Taking it back, I returned it to the table. Not wasting any time, I motioned for the group to follow me.

"Now, I will show your men to the horses they will use."

They followed me out of the receiving room, through the palace, and outside, where I saw the servant from earlier. He was holding the reins of two of the tallest, leanest, fastest horses. They stamped and whinnied when they saw me, then swished their tails back and forth. They knew a hard ride was coming, and they were ready. Just like their riders.

"Take the steeds and make haste," I ordered the guards. "Do not even think of returning here without those heads."

"Yes, my lord," they said. They mounted their rides, said a quick farewell to Lord Kane, and galloped off.

Having no further use for the elder Kane, I dismissed him with a backhanded wave and went back inside the palace, already imagining the end of the Strong bloodline. And that meddling Rook Cailean too.

With that task done, I could get to work on my other plan—ridding Faevenly of every last trace of humankind.

7

JULIO

A cool breeze swept over the meadow, sending the tops of the bright green grass leaning one way. When the breeze changed its course, the grass followed, now leaning the other way. Seated among the swaying stalks, I held my hand out, letting the thick blades tickle my skin with each sway, thinking life was perfect.

Celyse skipped into view, carrying a load of apples in her skirt. She smiled and plunked down beside me, then spread out her bounty before us. "Have you ever seen such red apples before?"

"I haven't," I admitted, examining the shiny fruit. "They are perfectly formed too. Not a bruise or a blemish."

She handed one to me, then took one for herself. I sank my teeth in, and juicy sweetness exploded in my mouth. "I don't think I've ever tasted one so sweet."

She was chewing a bite too, but managed a low moan. "So delicious."

I took another apple and examined it closely, thinking there was someone we needed to share it with but not remembering who. Swallowing my bite, I forced myself to sit still as I pushed my thoughts to the deepest parts of memory. Who was I forgetting? The thought lingered, just out of reach. Suddenly, a name drifted into my mind.

"Gabriela," I said almost in a whisper, my brain still processing. I met Celyse's confused stare. "Our daughter. Gabriela. We should save an apple for her."

Celyse furrowed her brow and tilted her head at me for a minute before she said, "Oh my, you are right. Our girl!" She shielded her eyes and glanced about the meadow. "Where is she?"

A twinge of panic set in, but when another breeze swept over us, I remembered. "I think she's doing homework."

Celyse lowered her hand, then considered me for a few long seconds. "That is right. She has a calculus test."

"Exactly," I agreed.

We finished our apples, savoring every last bite, and when we were done, we exhaled in quiet satisfaction. The half-eaten cores lay forgotten in the grass as we sank beside them, the earth cool and soft beneath our backs.

The meadow swayed around us, whispering with the wind. Celyse nestled closer, her warmth melting into mine, and I threaded my fingers through her long silver hair, letting the strands slip like silk through my hand. "I love you so much."

She looked at me with those magical green eyes

that always seemed to twinkle with affection. "I love you, too. With everything I am, I love you."

Taking her face in my hands, I kissed her with passion and tenderness, my emotions for her taking me completely. We had been through so much, and I still marveled at how we were even together and still alive. And I was grateful for every second with her.

When our kiss ended, she pulled away slowly. "What is it? I feel sadness coming from you."

"I feel it too, but I don't know what it is." I shrugged. "I'm sure it's nothing." Even as I said it, I knew it wasn't.

She smiled, then leapt to her feet. "I know the perfect thing to erase sadness." She held out her hand to help me up. "Fishing!"

I rose to my feet and matched her uplifted demeanor. "Great idea."

We had taken off our boots, but slipped them on quickly. Then, hand in hand, we started toward the edge of the meadow. We crossed through a thick hedge and made our way into a heavily wooded area filled with tall, skinny evergreen trees. The fine, needle-like grayish-green foliage provided so much shade it had erased all the grass, replacing it with dirt and leaves. A few more paces, and I began hearing the babbling creek. The farther into the woods we roamed, the louder the sound of the water grew until we came upon the flowing stream.

Here, the trees had thinned out, allowing brilliant

sun rays to flow in. Celyse smiled and closed her eyes, bringing her face up to meet the sunshine.

"I love it here," she said, releasing my hand so she could tie her skirt up at the knees and kick off her boots.

"I'll find some branches we can use for spears," I said, kicking off my boots too and tossing them with hers.

"I will help," she offered.

With her skirt tied up in a knot and her eyes on the ground, she picked her way over fallen branches as she followed the rippling, bubbling creek.

"Do not go too far, Celyse," I warned, my senses telling me to keep her close.

She climbed on a rock and lifted herself up on her toes. She craned her neck so she could see better. "The creek widens and turns into a river up ahead. Let us go see it!"

As I peered at the rippling clear water that stretched on, a tingle of fear connected at the back of my neck. It worked its way through me, telling me we should not go farther. That something awful lay ahead. Some sort of unknown danger. Something that would change our lives forever. I felt it with absolute certainty.

"Julio," Celyse beckoned, waving me over. "Come on."

She could not go. I would not let her. She meant too much to me.

My chest tightened, breath catching as a cold rush

swept through me. I didn't know what waited ahead—only that it was wrong. The air felt heavier there, thicker, as if the earth itself was warning us back. Every instinct screamed for me to stop her.

"Celyse! No!"

She froze, studied me for a few seconds, then climbed off the rock. She dashed over to me and held my hands. "What is it? What happened?"

I shook my head, my heart still racing. "I'm not sure. I just know that we can't go over there." I squeezed her hands. "Not ever."

She gazed at me with furrowed brows, as if trying to understand. But I had nothing to say that would help her. "You just need to believe me," I said, pulling her in for a hug. "Please." Don't go.

"I believe you," she said.

We stayed locked in our embrace for a long while, neither one of us wanting to let go of the other. "I could stay like this forever with you," I said, burying my face in her hair that smelled like the sweetest, freshest spring flowers.

She laughed and pulled away. "Then let us stay like this forever." She kissed me, then traced my face with her fingertips. "But can we also fish, maybe?" She pointed in the opposite direction from the river. "Over there?"

"Yes." I smiled. "Over there is fine."

We found a couple of branches perfect for spearing and spent the next few hours fishing to our heart's content. We made several great catches, laughing as we splashed in the creek and admired the beauty of the woods around us. I also did my best to steal as many kisses as I could from the woman I loved—and she was happy to supply them.

Yet every now and then, my gaze drifted downstream to where the water widened and the river began to form. Somewhere deep in my mind, buried in the part of me that dreamed and feared alike, I thought I knew what waited there.

And I knew the moment we saw it, everything would change.

8

GABRIELA

Over the next two days, our horses carried us away from the dirt and rock of the Sublands into a landscape of green grass and tall trees. My lungs and my nose were glad for the change, preferring air with more humidity over the rough dryness any day. And while Uncle Manny, Lady Sonia, and I had plenty of time to talk, it wasn't easy with the bumpy terrain, wind in our faces, and sun in our eyes. And at night, after a full day of riding, everyone slept fast and hard.

On our third day, the travel was really starting to take a toll and I wasn't sure if I could take much more of the strenuous galloping. Peering at Uncle Manny, I could tell he felt the same way. His face wore a pained grimace and his body looked crooked and strained.

"You okay, Uncle Manny?" I asked as our horses plodded along close together.

"No," he grumbled. "I miss my car, my bed, my shower, my house. My body can't take much more of this."

"I know. Me too." I wiped my sweaty brow with the back of my sleeve. "Even though I work out all the time because of fencing, this is nothing like that. I'm sore all over."

"Yeah, but you're young, *mija*. I'm not."

"Sorry, Uncle Manny."

"Nothing to be sorry about. It is what it is." He shielded his eyes as he gazed off into the distance. "Besides, I'm tough. I can take it. Though I do hope we get there soon," he said with a half smile.

"We are almost there," Rook called over his shoulder, riding a few paces ahead of us with Lady Sonia next to him. "Not much farther."

"Thank you, Jesus," Manny mumbled.

We settled back into silence again, and I started thinking about the last time I was at the Strong Haven West manor. We had gone for a meeting and Leaf had snapped Alexander Kane's neck. Now, the provinces wanted us dead. And the Strongs had lost the help of the Sublands.

"Are we doomed?" I asked Uncle Manny. "I feel like we're doomed."

His mouth fell open. "*¿Por qué dices eso?* We still have a chance. Especially with your Avila witchy skills. You can do stuff you haven't even imagined. There is hope for us still." He winked. "A lot of hope."

"I guess," I blew out.

I wanted to believe him, to let his hope sink into me, but it wouldn't take. Doubt had dug its claws in too deep. Every step of the horse carried us farther from safety, and I couldn't shake the feeling that we were riding toward the end of something we could never rebuild.

Lady Sonia slowed her horse and brought it to my other side. "Your parents believed in hope, Lady Gabriela. Even when it seemed like none existed. I too believe in hope. It lifts my spirits and brightens my days. It is also much better than the alternative."

"Well, hope is not a strategy," I pointed out.

Uncle Manny frowned. "Who said that?"

"Mr. Hillyer. My history teacher from school."

"This Mr. Hillyer teacher sounds wise," Lady Sonia said. "Hope is entirely different from a strategy. To succeed in any endeavor, one needs both—hope *and* strategy. They coexist. So he is correct. One is not the other."

I thought her point was a good one, but it didn't make me feel any better. "Well, I guess that makes things even worse for us, because I don't feel like we have either of those things."

"There is hope beyond that small mountain ridge," Rook said, pointing off into the distance.

I narrowed my eyes and searched the mountain that resembled a profile of a man with a heavy brow and a pointed nose. "Looks like a face," I said, marveling at the facade.

"It does," Lady Sonia confirmed. "Beyond that, the terrain will flatten, and you will see the manor house."

The idea of a house with a bath and a bed and a meal brightened my state of mind, pushing away all thoughts of hopelessness and despair. Our horses must've sensed the elevated mood too. They picked up speed and galloped at a quicker pace. True to Rook's assessment, we crossed the ridge and the manor house popped into view. With the sun descending and the orange and purple rays outlining the house, it looked like a promise of salvation, a true paradise.

"Oh my gosh, yes," I uttered.

We galloped with excitement, moving so fast I had to squint my eyes against the blasting wind. A few minutes more and we were there.

Uncle Manny slid off his horse as quickly as he could, cradling his back and walking around the circular stone driveaway. "I said it before and I'll say it again, horseback riding sucks."

Two translucent figures came out from behind the back of the manor, laughing. "He did say that before."

It was the two dead fae that were friends of Leto's. "Ferna and Parlan are here," I said.

"Ferna and Parlan?" Uncle Manny asked, whipping his stare in the direction I was looking. "Have y'all been here at the manor this whole time?"

"Since we were killed when Draven collapsed the manor on us?" Ferna asked. "Yes, we have."

I faced Uncle Manny. "Draven collapsed the manor on them?"

"On all of us. Ferna and I, and a few others, did not make it out," Parlan explained.

"Yeah," Uncle Manny said, rubbing the back of his neck. "It was pretty awful. A few others died too, including Lady Wren's husband."

My mouth parted in surprise. "Lady Wren's husband?" My stomach dropped.

The door to the stately home that resembled a smaller version of the palace in the east swung open, revealing Lady Wren. She wore a long black gown and had her silver hair twisted up in a tight bun. Now I understood her somber mood, and her choice of color for her dress. She wore black the last time I visited too.

"Lady Gabriela," she said with a formal nod. She looked at the others and offered them nods too. "Lady Sonia, Lord Rook, and Lord Manny, please come in. I have been expecting you all. Lord Adrius sent news of your arrival with a raven courier."

"Thank you, Lady Wren," Lady Sonia said with a bow.

"Thank you very much," I added.

Two fae dressed in black took the reins of our horses and led them away. I dusted off my pants and brushed my long hair out of my face, then followed everyone inside. Lady Wren ushered us into the all-marble foyer where four maid servants were waiting with trays of juice, fruit, cheese, and bread. My mouth gushed because we'd only had water and fruit flats for days. And not a lot of it.

"Oh, Lady Wren," I said, going for a handful of berries. "Thank you so much."

Uncle Manny shoved a chunk of cheese in his mouth. "This is delicious. Thank you," he mumbled with a full mouth. Then he motioned to one of the trays of food. "Can I hold that?"

The maid servant didn't know how to respond, but with no objection from Lady Wren, she handed the tray over.

"Thanks," Uncle Manny said, taking it with a swoop while he continued munching.

Lady Sonia and Rook helped themselves to a few bites while Lady Wren bowed her head in acknowledgment and explained the setup. "I realize there is much to discuss and much to do, but I recommend a bath and a fresh change of clothes for each of you and a good night's sleep. We can meet early in the morning to discuss our predicament." She motioned to the maid servants. "I have assigned one servant for each of you. They will escort you to your rooms at once and will see to anything you need."

I didn't have to smell myself to know I definitely needed a bath, plus a soft bed to crash on. My body throbbed with pain, and I was beyond exhausted.

"My gratitude for your hospitality," Rook said to Lady Wren. Then he said to us, "We will meet back here at dawn."

We were led by the maid servants up the marble staircase, then split off in pairs. When we reached the landing, Lady Sonia and I were led to the right, and Uncle Manny and Rook were led to the left.

With all the marble with flecks of gold and the tall pedestals adorned with crystal vases filled with the brightest flowers, it really did feel like the palace in the east. Only smaller.

"When this structure was demolished," Lady Sonia

explained, "Malena, your mother's half sister, rebuilt this place to be an exact replica of the palace in the east. But on a smaller scale."

"I can see that," I said, admiring all the detail. "It's amazing."

My thoughts stayed on Malena. With all the truths I'd been discovering about my family, I wanted to know more about her. Especially since my parents never talked about her. "Lady Sonia, what was she like? Malena?"

The maid servant stopped at one of the doors and said in a tiny voice, "Your bedchamber, Lady Gabriela."

I held up a finger, letting the maid servant know I needed a second, and stepped closer to Sonia. "Was she... terrible?"

Lady Sonia drew in a deep breath and held it for a few long seconds before answering. "She was a lot like her mother, misguided and power hungry."

"Oh," I said. "So... pretty terrible then."

Lady Sonia placed her hand on my arm. "It is of no import, my lady. You are nothing like her. You are like your mother, honorable and true."

I nodded, not really knowing what to say because my mom and Malena shared a father. How much of him was misguided and power hungry? And how much of that was buried somewhere deep inside of me?

"You will feel better after a bath and a night of slumber in a comfortable bed," she assured me. "We all will."

"You're right. Thank you, Lady Sonia. Good night."

Lady Sonia continued on with her maid servant. The one with me opened the door and moved to the side. "After you, my lady."

As I stepped into the bedchamber, the aroma of lavender, rose, and gardenia wafted over me. My shoulders instantly dropped and my neck relaxed as I breathed in the soothing scents, letting them work their way through me as I scanned the large open room.

Tall arched windows lined one side of the room. They were open, allowing a soft breeze to flow through the space and rustling the pure white drapes that framed each side. To the left was a large four-poster bed with intricate vine-carved rich wood columns, one in each corner that supported an upper panel of the same white fabric that adorned the windows. A plush pink sofa, a coffee table, and two brown leather chairs sat on the other side of the room. Beyond that was a white marble tub that looked more like a large hot tub.

"Wow, this room is huge," I marveled.

"This is the largest room in the manor, for the lady of the house."

The lady of the house?

The maid servant caught on to my bewildered stare and explained, "Lady Gabriela of House Strong. You are the lady of the house."

"Oh yeah," I mumbled. "I guess I am."

She held up the silver tray she still carried, and I took a handful of grapes. I plopped them in my mouth and made my way to the tub. Rose petals and gardenias floated along the top of the lavender-colored water. The maid servant set her tray on a nearby table within reach of the tub, then motioned to another table on the other side.

"You will find everything you need for washing on that table." Then she gave a small bow. "I will return when you are finished."

She walked away and exited behind a door that blended in with the ivory walls. When it closed all the way, I made a beeline for the food, popping handfuls of berries in my mouth and savoring the fresh juices, followed by chunks of cheese and bread. After several servings and with my hunger satisfied, I stripped off my filthy clothes and sat on the edge of the tub. I dipped one toe in to test the water. Finding the temperature perfectly warm, I slid into the refreshing and soothing waters with a soft plunge.

Below the surface of the water, my body relaxed, my mind eased, and the urgency of everything we'd been through moved to the back of my mind, but didn't stay there long.

What were we going to do now that the Sublands had turned us away?

I shut off my thoughts, unable to deal with all that, and broke the water. Searching for a distraction, I waded across the tub to the table with the bath products and found a dark purple bar of soap with herbal leaves and bits of flower petals. I brought it to my nose and inhaled.

"Ah, lavender," I said with a smile.

Next to that was a bowl of white lotion and a comb made out of a seashell. I swiped my finger through the lotion and took a deep inhale. "Coconut." I breathed in deeper. "And vanilla."

I got busy sudsing up the bar, then rubbed the lather all over my body. Bursts of lavender and clove filled my nose, leaving me with an overwhelming sense of peace and calm while also making my skin super soft. After that, I massaged the lotion in my hair, then rinsed it off with several dips under the water.

When I finished, I leaned back against the tub and closed my eyes. Even though I had been in the water for a while, it was still so nice and warm. As much as I wanted to stay in the comforting bath and enjoy the lapping water against my skin and the soothing scents, I was two seconds away from falling asleep.

Glancing around, I spotted a plush white towel on the edge of the tub. I got out of the water and started drying myself. Wrapping the towel around my body, I searched for my bag but didn't see it. Instead, I saw a long white silk nightgown on my bed with a set of matching underwear.

I spun around, looking for the maid servant, but didn't see her. She must've been in and out while my head was under the water. Not that it mattered. The maid servants were always so quick and quiet.

I put on the silky-smooth undergarments, then followed that with the gown that fit perfectly.

"May I turn your bed down?"

A small gasp escaped my lips because I hadn't heard the maid servant enter the room, but there she was, standing at the foot of my bed. "You can't sneak up on people like that," I said with a hand over my heart.

"My lady, I did not mean to startle you. And I did not mean to sneak," she said, mortified. "My deepest apologies."

"It's okay," I said with an apologetic smile, lowering my hand. "Y'all are just so stealthy."

"Y'all?" She blinked. "I do not know what that is."

"Oh," I laughed. "It's a contraction for *you all*."

She blinked again. "Contraction?"

Everyone in Faevenly spoke formally, and nobody used contractions. But it didn't dawn on me that they actually didn't know what a contraction was. "Um, a contraction is when two words are joined together. So *you* and *all* together is *y'all*."

"Y'all," she said. When the word came out, she covered her mouth and laughed. "That is funny like that."

"Yep," I laughed. "It actually really is."

There were so many magical things about Faevenly I didn't understand and were never explained, and it wasn't just the language. It was so much more, like the orbs that floated around and provided light, the water that appeared in the tub when I bathed, and then magically drained when I finished... with no drain. Not to mention the fact that while the weather varied some, it was still always perfect with no bugs. And the servants hardly made a sound.

I eyed the dainty maiden in front of me. "What is your name?"

"Lillian, my Lady."

I smiled. "I love that name. Thank you, Lillian."

She motioned toward the bed. "May I turn your bed down?"

"No, that's okay. I can do that myself."

"Very well. Is there anything else you need?"

"No, I'm fine. Thank you for everything."

She nodded and said with a smile, "Y'all are welcome."

I thought of stopping her and explaining how y'all was plural, but I thought it might be confusing. That, and I was way too tired for a long explanation of anything.

She left my room as quietly as she entered, and the floating orb lights dimmed to darkness. I wasted no time pulling down the soft white bedspread and climbing into bed. The crisp and cool sheets made me feel like I was floating on air, and the pillow cradled my head perfectly. I turned to my side and snuggled my hands together under my head, then stared at the tree branches swaying outside my window.

Alone and exhausted, I felt despair and hopelessness creep up to the surface once again. But this time, instead of thinking of the Sublands or my parents, I thought of Leaf. I hadn't tried to reach him with my mind because I'd been afraid. What if he really was the enemy? What if I found out he didn't care for me and was only using me? What if I tried to reach him and

Draven was near and somehow attacked me and the others?

Fear kept me from finding out the truth about Leaf, but if all was lost for us, for me, why not know why he did what he did? What was the worst that could happen to me?

I was about to find out.

9

GABRIELA

With my eyes closed, I pictured Leaf in my mind. Beautiful, complicated, with deep blue eyes, long dark hair, full lips, a tall and lean muscular body, and a smooth deep voice. Despite everything, he had worked his way deep into my heart. And I was determined to find out his truth.

Keeping my thoughts steady on his image, a pleasing tingle started swirling inside me. It grew with each breath until it rushed through me like a tidal wave. Weightlessness swept over me, sending me into a free fall. I stayed like that for a few long seconds until my feet met a solid surface.

Afraid of what I might find, I crouched low and slowly opened my eyes.

Darkness surrounded me, like a snug blanket. I waited for my eyes to adjust to my surroundings, and a hazy, dim light filtered into view. I followed the glow and looked up to see a small opening way overhead and thought for sure I was standing at the bottom of a well.

Bringing my gaze back down, I scanned the stone walls around me until I noticed a person sitting on the ground. I didn't have to look twice to recognize Leaf. His long legs were pulled up and his arms were wrapped around his knees. His head rested against his forearms.

I moved closer to him, lowering myself to sit, and his head snapped up. His eyes widened. His mouth parted. "Gabriela?"

"Leaf," I smiled.

He reached out to me, but his hands passed right through me. "How?" he asked with a shake of his head. "How are you here?"

"It's something I can do," I said.

"Magic. From your witch father."

"Yes. From my father and grandmother." Scooting closer to him, I saw blood on his hands and cuts on his face. "You're hurt!"

He shook his head. "I am fine." He reached out to me but his hand swiped through mine. "Did you receive my message from the sprite? Is that why you are here?"

"A sprite?" I tilted my head. "What are you talking about?"

"She has not yet arrived," he muttered under his breath. "Never mind that," he said quickly. "There is much I need to say to you."

My heart splintered at the sight of him—the shadows, the cuts, the agony. "You don't have to," I whispered. "I already know."

Even as I said it, I felt it deep inside me—he'd

never meant to hurt me. Whatever he'd done, whatever he'd become, it wasn't truly him.

"I must, Gabriela," he pleaded. "I must say the words." His blue eyes glistened with emotion. "I wronged you and all of Strong Haven. I caused many deaths." His words broke and he shook his head with a swallow. "But you must know, that while it was my hand that did it, my hand did not belong to me. You must believe me."

Seeing him like this made it hard to breathe. I wanted nothing more than to wrap my arms around him and feel him next to me, to tell him everything was okay, but I couldn't. Instead, I held my hazy hands to his solid face.

"I know, Leaf. I know. It was Draven. I know he compelled you."

"Draven," he repeated with alarm in his eyes. He scooted close. "Gabriela, you are in grave danger. All of you are. Draven has assassins—"

A gust of air blasted through the small dark space, sending a rush of tingly fear through my body. Leaf narrowed his eyes at something behind me, then slammed his hands against my shoulders. The force hit me straight through to my bones, shoving me out of the darkness and sending me tumbling. I jumped, my eyes flying open, my heart thudding against my chest as I rolled out of bed and landed with a crash on the marble floor.

"What in the hell?" I panted, holding my hand over

the cross that hung around my neck as the orbs in the room brightened.

"Lady Gabriela!" Lillian pattered over to me. She gasped when she saw me on the floor, then reached out to help me up. "My lady, are you all right?"

"Yes," I said, catching my breath. "I'm fine."

My body shook from the fear I had felt and the terror I had seen in Leaf's eyes, not to mention the fact that he had actually shoved me out of our mind connection. I lowered myself onto the edge of the bed and was working to steady myself when my door flew open.

"What was that?" Lady Sonia asked. She wore a red robe over a white nightgown and hurried over to me. Her long dark hair hung loose down her back. "What was that quake?"

"You felt that?" I asked.

Rook dashed in, brandishing a dagger. He circled the room, looking behind the furniture and the curtains. "What was that tremble?"

"You felt it too?" I asked.

"Maid Lillian," Sonia said with a formal nod. "Thank you for your attention to Lady Gabriela, but we can handle things from here."

Lillian bowed, looking scared to death. "Yes, my lady."

The slender maid servant took a robe draped over her arm that I hadn't even noticed and handed it to me. She skittered away, leaving me alone with Lady Sonia and Rook. A second later, Lady Wren swept into the room.

"What is going on?" the stately custodian asked, surveying the room. "The entire manor house shook."

"We are here for that reason. And we do not yet know what is going on," Lady Sonia answered. "Though Lady Gabriela is about to tell us."

Slipping on the robe, I tied it around my waist with shaky hands. "I-I used my mind connection abilities to find Leaf." I paused to see if they had a response, but they didn't. Not yet, anyway. "He was in a dark place with stone walls and a stone floor. Overhead was a small opening. I think he was down in a well."

"A well?" Rook asked.

"Yes," I nodded, pausing in case he had any more questions, but he didn't, so I went on. "His hands were bloodied and his face was cut, and he was sitting alone in the dark."

"Was he able to see you?" Lady Sonia asked.

"Yes, he saw me. He spoke to me too. He told me how sorry he was about everything and said he wasn't in control of himself. Then he told me that I was in grave danger, saying Draven had assassins, but before he could finish his sentence, something happened." I paused, my mind replaying every detail of our interaction. "A cold blast of air swept through the dark space and an eerie feeling overcame me. Like a massive energy shift, something terrible and dreadful."

"Draven," Lady Sonia uttered.

"Had to have been," I agreed. "Leaf felt it too. His eyes narrowed on something behind me and then he slammed his hands against my shoulders and physically hurled me out of our connection and back here to my room."

Lady Sonia's mouth parted with shock. "Leaf pushed you out of your mind connection with him?"

I nodded. "Yes."

But Rook's focus was on something else entirely. His nostrils flared and his eyes blazed with anger. "Assassins?"

"Yes," I gulped. "He said Draven has assassins."

Lady Wren looked taken aback. "Here?" She looked around at all of us. "Do you think he meant here?"

I shrugged. "I don't know. I mean, maybe? Or coming here?"

"Thunderation," Rook growled under his breath. "It is no longer safe here."

My heart lurched. "Now? It's not safe... right now?" I clutched the top of my gown, then realized my uncle wasn't in the room. "Oh no. Where's Uncle Manny?"

Rook practically flew out of the room, and the rest of us followed. His boots thudded angrily against the marble floor as we rushed down the hall and to the rooms on the other side of the stairs. He flung open one of the doors, sending the floating orbs flaring to life. The glow revealed Uncle Manny fast asleep. Mouth open, drool dripping, his arm hanging off the side of the bed.

I exhaled. "Oh, thank goodness." I placed my hands on his back and nudged him. "Uncle Manny, wake up."

He mumbled, then cracked open his eyes. It took him a few seconds to focus and realize a small group had gathered around his bed. He bolted upright. "What's wrong?"

"Draven has assassins. And we need to leave," Rook said. "Now."

Uncle Manny shot a confused look my way, so I explained quickly. "I did the mind connection thing with Leaf and he told me."

He ran his fingers through his hair. "You did?"

Lady Wren turned with a swish and headed for the door. "I will make the necessary arrangements."

Manny climbed out of bed and Rook started barking orders. "We pack up and head into the forest and figure out the rest later. Make haste with preparations. We do not have time to spare."

With that, he left the room, leaving me with Lady Sonia, Uncle Manny, and a double-knotted stomach.

Manny reached out and squeezed my arm. "Go get ready, and I'll do the same."

Lady Sonia and I went back to our rooms to change clothes and get our things. When I stepped into mine, Lillian had already started gathering my stuff. My bag lay open on my bed, and an outfit of green pants and a black shirt was set out with tall black boots.

Lillian motioned to the outfit. "This clothing is good for riding, and the coloring will serve you well in the forest."

"Thank you, Lillian." My pulse quickened. Every second we lingered felt dangerous—like the walls themselves were holding their breath, waiting for the assassins to strike.

"I will leave you to change your clothing and will return when you are finished," she said.

With my nerves still rocked from my encounter with Leaf, I untied my robe with shaky hands, tossed it on the bed, and got dressed in a hurry. Sitting on the floor with the plush white rug underneath me, I yanked on my boots and started lacing them up.

So many emotions and feelings swirled inside of me—grief over missing my mom and dad, heartache after seeing Leaf hurt and alone, and terror over what he had said about Draven. I ran my fingers through the soft rug and whispered a prayer. "Please let us make it out of here okay."

A soft knock sounded on my door. "*Mija*, it's me. Uncle Manny."

"Come in."

He came in and walked over to me. The fine lines across his forehead seemed deeper than usual, and puffy dark circles encased his eyes. I even thought he was limping a little. He held out his hand and helped me up.

"Are you okay? You look kinda..."

He waved his hands. "I'm fine. Don't worry about me. But let's hurry and get outta here."

With our bags in tow, we quickly made our way downstairs to the foyer and found Lady Sonia and Rook packed up and ready to go. Lady Wren was there too.

"We have fresh horses and supplies for each of you," she said, "along with the items Lady Sonia requested."

"Items?" I asked.

"Herbs, tinctures, and oils," Lady Sonia explained.

My mom kept a cabinet filled with herbs and leaves and oils, as did my *abuela*. I thought it was probably a good idea for Sonia to have that stuff too. Though I hoped we wouldn't need it.

"We must get moving," Rook ordered.

I was about to pick up my bag when Lady Sonia froze in place. She raised her finger to her lips, signaling everyone to be quiet.

Rook pulled me and Uncle Manny close, tucking us behind him. "What do you hear?" he asked her in a whisper.

"I hear a flutter," Lady Sonia whispered.

"I do as well," Lady Wren added, keeping still as her eyes darted about.

We huddled close together, unsure of what was happening, when a tiny flying figure flitted into the room.

"A wood sprite," Lady Sonia said in wonder.

Wood sprite? I shot her a look. "Leaf said he sent a sprite to me. This must be it."

The sprite had skin like tree bark with shiny gold wings, yellow eyes, and yellow moss for hair that started at her head and traveled down her back. She circled around us a few times.

"I am looking for a lady called Gabriela," she announced in a high-pitched voice.

I met Uncle Manny's surprised eyes, then slowly raised my hand. "I'm Gabriela."

The sprite twirled and came closer to me, hovering at eye level and wearing a serious expression. "I am Majestic and I have a dire message from a lovely fae named Leaf with midnight hair and ocean eyes. He says you are in danger, that assassins are coming, and for you to leave this place at once. He says to be careful."

A cold weight settled in my chest. Our assumption was right. The assassins were coming. "Thank you, Majestic. I saw him at the bottom of a well not long ago. He told me you were coming."

She shook her tiny head. "He is not at the bottom of a well. He is being held by an evil being in the Strong Haven Palace dungeon in the east."

"Strong Haven dungeon?" My stomach dropped. Leaf was Draven's prisoner. But also that meant Draven had Strong Haven East. Did he also have Leto and the others?

"Oh no," Uncle Manny muttered.

Rook turned and slammed his hands against the wall. "Draven has taken Strong Haven East, and we are in danger!"

Lady Sonia pressed her fingers to her mouth. "Leto," she muttered with worry. She lowered her hand and asked the tiny sprite. "What of the people of the palace? Are they still there or did they get out in time?"

"I do not know, my lady," Majestic said with downcast eyes. "I am only charged with the delivery of my message. My apologies for not knowing more. And now, I must take my leave. This is all very frightening."

She bowed low, then twirled and zoomed away.

Rook seethed and marched around the room with heavy steps. "No telling what Draven is up to. But whatever it is, we are not safe here."

"Agreed. You all must hurry," Lady Wren rushed out. "And do not worry about Lord Leto; I will send messages and see what I can find out."

A tingle of fear gathered at the back of my neck. I stilled, then rubbed the spot, when Ferna and Parlan dashed through the wall. "Two horses riding fast have arrived! The riders are armed and coming to the front of the manor!"

"What is it?" Lady Sonia asked, following my line of sight.

A chill ripped through me. "It's Ferna and Parlan." My hands shook. "They say two armed men are coming to the door."

Rook drew his dagger and held it out, then said to Lady Wren, "Go someplace safe and take Gabriela, Manny and Sonia. I will handle our visitors."

"No, Rook. I can fight!" I asserted, holding my ground despite the fear coursing through me.

"I can too," Uncle Manny added.

"As can I," Lady Sonia said.

With no time for debate, Rook drew his fighting stick from the sheath at his back and thrust it at me.

Lady Wren must've had a dagger on her, because she handed one to Uncle Manny. A fierce expression crossed Lady Sonia's face as she lifted her skirt and pulled out her own dagger, which was strapped to her thigh.

"Behind me," Rook directed in a low tone, his voice sounding deadly and strong.

We took our places behind Rook as Lady Wren and the maid servants scurried away. Rook's hulking form readied with his feet wide and shoulders squared. Uncle Manny raised his dagger next to me, and Lady Sonia did the same on the other side. With my heart hammering, I raised my stick and gripped it with all my strength.

Ferna and Parlan floated forward. With their bodies on our side of the door, they moved their heads through the wood. "Now!" Ferna called.

"Now!" I shouted.

The door busted open with a thwack and two fae in all black shot through like cannons. Rook rushed at one with a battle cry, their daggers clashing, while the other charged for me. Uncle Manny lunged with his weapon, and I lashed out with my stick. The attacker parried and spun with ease, knocking us off balance as Uncle Manny and I collided.

Lady Sonia swooped in next with a graceful turn, slicing her dagger across the attacker's cheek. Blood gushed from the spot as he swung his own dagger, barely missing her throat. With an angry growl, he jumped and kicked, landing his boot square against her shoulder. She crashed against the wall, then slumped to the ground.

"Hey!" I hollered, drawing the deadly fae away from Lady Sonia. "Over here!"

He spun, his eyes filled with wrath as he raised his dagger and chucked it. I ducked in time for the black onyx weapon to soar over me and lodge into the wall over my head.

"You are dead," my attacker hissed. Blood dripping down his pale face, he ran forward.

"Gabriela, the sweep!" Manny shouted.

The sweep! It was a move he and my dad had taught me once when we were sparring in the backyard. I clutched my stick like a baseball bat, then lunged and swung at the attacker's lower legs. He stumbled, and Uncle Manny lowered his head and tackled him from behind like a linebacker. They crashed to the ground with a thud.

"Manny, move!" Rook yelled.

He rolled away, clearing the way for Rook to pounce and drive his dagger through the attacker's chest.

Backing away with my stick raised, scanning for the other attacker, I saw Rook had already taken care of him. He was sprawled out on the floor, eyes wide, mouth open. Blood seeped from his head, spreading out all over the marble floor.

"Don't look, *mija*," Uncle Manny said, hugging me and turning me away. But it was too late. I had seen it all.

"I'm fine," I said to him in the calmest voice I could muster, not wanting him to know how freaked out I was. "Help Lady Sonia."

He left me and dashed over to her, giving her a hand to help her up. "Are you okay?" he asked her.

"Yes, thank you," she said.

"We must go," Rook declared, up on his feet now and inspecting the bodies, as if making sure they were really dead. "At once."

Lady Wren swept back in with the maid servants at her heels. Her lips were pursed and her brow furrowed. "Go now," she warned. "Before any others show up."

I stepped closer to her. "But what about you?"

"I will be fine. I always am, my lady. Now go!"

We hurried outside, where our horses waited under the night sky. I still had Rook's fighting stick and wanted to keep it in case we were attacked again. Before I could ask him, he must've thought the same thing because he slipped off his sheath and secured it to my back, then placed the stick inside. He looked to Uncle Manny, who still had Lady Wren's dagger. He unbuckled the holster around his waist and handed it over.

"Stay sharp," he said to us. "There could be more."

With our weapons in place, we secured our things and mounted our rides. The magnificent beasts whinnied and snorted, their eyes wide with fear and excitement. Glancing at Uncle Manny, I saw fear in his eyes too, but more than that he looked in pain.

He flashed me a strained smile. "I got it," he assured me. "*Estoy bien.*"

We rode hard, hooves pounding against the stone path as we tore away from the manor. Moonlight streaked through the canopy, silvering the trees and flashing over our faces as we veered into the woods. The wind whipped past, carrying the scent of crushed pine and damp earth. We pressed faster, weaving between trunks and ducking under low branches, the shadows closing in around us.

But my thoughts refused to stay on the path ahead. They went to Leaf—trapped in Strong Haven's dungeon. I could almost feel his pain through the darkness, like a distant echo calling out to me. Whatever Draven was doing to him, it had to be unbearable.

I tightened my grip on the reins, jaw clenched, a surge of determination burning through the ache in my chest. No matter how strong that witch's hold was on Leaf, I would find a way to break it. And once I did, I'd end Draven once and for all... I had to.

10

LEAF

Draven's sinister presence exploded into the cave during my mind connection with Gabriela, looming behind her like a deadly tidal wave. I had to protect her. I slammed my hands against her shoulders, meeting a surge of warmth as her shimmery form whisked out of the darkness.

Draven swept into the space she had occupied, his cloak snapping behind him. Moonlight poured through the opening above, striking his crystal eyes—cold and furious.

"Where is she?" he bellowed, voice shaking the air. "Where?!"

"Away from the likes of you," I snarled, forcing myself upright.

His rage coalesced—raw power swirling around his hands, red and pulsing like molten light. He flung it at me. The blast hit hard. My back slammed against the wall. The air ripped from my lungs.

"You dare defy me?" He jerked his hands back and forth, sending stabbing pain crisscrossing my body as though he were dragging a multitude of daggers over my skin, each one tearing deeper into me.

I pushed off the wall and lunged for him, pure instinct driving me forward, but he cut me off with a wave as another surge of red magic threw me back like a broken puppet. "I own you, Leaf of the Sublands! Body and soul, you are mine!"

The words split through me. The power followed. Vision shattered. Sound collapsed. The world dissolved into flashes of red and black—his laughter, my scream—until everything caved inward.

I could not see. Could not hear. Could not even comprehend what Draven was doing to me.

I hit the ground hard, blood on my tongue.

Then silence.

11

GABRIELA

W e galloped through the woods for what seemed like hours, each up and down motion sending pain through my body. My thighs, my butt, my arms, and even my face hurt. As if sensing how tired we were, or maybe it was on Rook's orders, our horses slowed to a steady trot.

"Finally," I muttered, shifting around in my saddle.

The stamping of hooves against dirt and leaves droned in the background of my mind while a soft breeze swirled around me like a blanket. The combo made me even more tired, and I must've fallen asleep because suddenly my head lolled with a jerk, and drool rolled down my chin. My arms were so weak I didn't even wipe the spittle away. Instead, I gave in to my exhaustion and leaned over, resting against the base of the horse's neck.

Threading my fingers through its mane, I whispered, "Don't let me fall, boy." And then I added, "Or girl. Okay? Because that would really suck."

Snuggled up against the horse's thick, soft coat, I closed my eyes so sleep could take me, but before it settled in, I heard Lady Sonia.

"There," she said. "Everyone, let us camp over there for the night."

The horses plodded on a few more steps before coming to a halt. Instead of dismounting, I stayed in place, my body unable to move.

"Gabriela," Uncle Manny called out. "We've stopped, *mija*."

His words worked their way through me, forcing me to lift my head. We had come upon a clearing circled by tall thin trees. Sitting up, I dragged my legs to the side of the saddle, then slid off my horse.

"I'll set up our pallets," Uncle Manny said.

"I'll help," I mumbled, prying myself away from my horse and joining him as he shuffled through the bags. With our pallets out, we spread them on the ground, then tossed the blankets on top.

"I have to sleep," I mumbled, crawling onto the nearest pallet and pulling the blanket over my body.

WHEN I WAS LITTLE AND STRESSED OUT OR SAD OR angry, my parents would say a good night's sleep would make things better. They were always right. But in this case, when I woke up on the ground under a blanket in the middle of the forest with the morning sun trickling down on me, their theory was proved wrong.

Nothing was better.

A fire burned in the middle of our small camp. On either side of the flames were wood poles that held another wood pole that stretched across the fire and held a small black pot. Lady Sonia sat close, watching whatever she was cooking. Rook wasn't around, and Uncle Manny was still next to me, sleeping.

I got up with a yawn and stretched my arms, then went into the woods to do my morning business. When I returned, I sat next to Lady Sonia and joined her in watching the pot.

"What are you making?" I asked, yawning and rubbing my eyes.

"A potion for Manny."

I blinked. "A potion? What kind of potion?"

She stood and tossed some leaves in the pot, then gave it a stir with a long stick. "I have been noticing his difficulties with our journey, so I concocted a potion to help him with his aches and pains."

"Whoa, really?" I whiffed the steam from the pot, smelling dirt and leaves.

"Yes. His muscles will be soothed and rejuvenated, as if he were the young man he was the first time he was here." She kept stirring. "It will help him immensely while he journeys."

"Incredible," I whispered. I nodded at her bag filled with packets and vials. "Is that the stuff you got from Lady Wren?"

"It is. I have been using some of the items for my potion. I also spent some time gathering things this morning. As a matter of fact, Rook is out now hunting for basil."

"Basil?" My brows raised. "We use that to prepare Italian food back home."

"It is most delicious and edible, but in large doses and combined with the correct ingredients, it can reverse the visible signs of aging."

Reverse aging? Now that was something. "What kind of correct ingredients?"

"Ingredients that are only found in the fae realm, such as water from the Green Falls."

"Oh yeah, the healing water," I said.

She lifted a small bottle of the thick green liquid from her bag and poured some into the pot. It sparked when it hit the mixture, and a trail of green smoke wafted into the air.

"Wow," I muttered. "Is it supposed to do that?"

"Yes," she answered. "It means it is working. Now I am only waiting for—"

"I am here," Rook announced, tramping back into camp with an entire basil plant in his arms, roots, dirt, and all.

He handed the bush to Lady Sonia, and clumps of dirt sprinkled on her skirt. She inspected the plant, then plucked the leaves one by one and dropped several in the pot. When she finished, she scooped up the dirt from her skirt and sprinkled it in. Then she stirred everything around. She stepped back and dusted herself off.

"It is ready," she declared. "When Manny awakes, I will serve it for him."

"Uh... you put dirt in it," I said with a curious look, as if making sure she knew what she had done.

"I did," she smiled. "It will amplify the potion and help it work faster."

"Let us wake him now, then. We do not have all day," Rook huffed.

He started walking toward the pallets, but I stopped him short with a tug of his arm. "I'll do it."

Uncle Manny needed to wake up, but not by a hard shake from Rook. I went over to my uncle and crouched down low. "Hey, Uncle Manny." I tapped his shoulder. "You need to get up. Lady Sonia has something for you."

The long days of travel had really caught up with him, not to mention the fight with those guys back at the manor. It took him a while to open his eyes. "What? Something for me?"

"Yeah, get up and come see."

He sat up with a groan and slowly rose to his feet, stretching and groaning some more. "Give me a minute." After a quick detour into the woods, he came back looking awake but still drained.

"Good morning, everyone," he said, joining us by the fire where the pot was.

"Manny," Lady Sonia said. "I have fashioned a potion to help you regain strength and vitality, like you had when you were younger."

He perked up. "You did?"

She stirred the contents with a stick. "Yes, I did. It

will help you with your soreness and discomfort and will make traveling much easier."

"I'll take two, please," he laughed.

She smiled, then took a large cup from her bag. She reached into the pot and submerged it under the liquid. She brought it out and handed it to Manny.

"Here you go, my friend. Drink it all, please."

He carefully placed his hands around the cup, his eyes opening wide with surprise. "I thought the cup would be hot, but it's not." He examined the contents of the cup, then peered into the pot and saw that there was some left. "I probably need all of it. My back is really killing me."

Rook took the pot and poured the rest in his cup. "There," he said. "Every last drop."

"Thanks, Rook."

Manny blew on the liquid, then brought the cup to his face and whiffed. "Hey, it doesn't smell so bad." He lowered the cup and said to me, "Once, your Uncle Leto gave me and your dad some sort of concoction that looked and smelled like piss."

Lady Sonia crossed her arms and chuckled. "This will not taste like that. I assure you."

"Leto's drink worked, so I'm sure this one will too," he went on. "And I need all the medicinal help I can get right now." He raised the glass, took a deep breath and said. "Here goes nothing."

He brought the cup to his lips, took a small sip, and swallowed. Licking his lips a little, he raised his brows in a pleasing way, then drank the rest in a few large gulps.

"Ahhh," he said, wiping his mouth. "That was actually tasty, like liquid pizza. Thank you, Sonia."

"You are most welcome," she said, taking the empty cup.

Uncle Manny patted his legs. "Now what?"

"Yeah," I said, studying my uncle, waiting for some sort of visible transformation. "When will it kick in?"

"I did not have the exact measurement of things, and I had to improvise some ingredients and forgo others, but the potion takes time in the best of circumstances. However, I do believe the effects will be felt by tonight."

Uncle Manny smiled. "If my aches and pains will really disappear, then I certainly don't mind waiting a day. Heck, even two days."

"With that settled, we should continue on," Rook prodded. "It is best to not stay in one place too long."

Although I admired and appreciated the hulking fae's tenacity and his unwavering desire to protect me, I had no idea if he even knew where he wanted to go because really, there was no safe place for us. I eased myself down onto a rock and started playing with a stick.

"Where can we go from here, Rook? Draven has the east, the west is not safe, and the Sublands don't want us. Not to mention the other provinces are standing with Draven. So in case you haven't noticed, there's really nowhere for us to go."

Rook stilled. He stayed like that for a few long seconds before saying in a low voice, "I confess I do not know."

Uncle Manny let out a huge sigh and sat down too. Lady Sonia joined in. Still playing with my stick, I watched the nearby grazing horses as birds soared from tree to tree, chirping as if everything was right in the world. But I knew the truth. Nothing was right.

Leaf was locked away in a dungeon, Leto was probably being held too. Not to mention my parents in the Passing Place. We had no move left.

"You know," Uncle Manny said. "Whenever there was an issue at work, your dad would always say to work the problem." He scratched his head. "So, let's work the problem."

I traced my stick around the dirt and leaves. "The problem... that seems kinda big right now. Doesn't it?"

"It is not as big as you think," Lady Sonia said. "The problem is simply Draven. He is deadly and powerful, and we do not even know how deadly he has become now that he has the aquoise."

"Actually, you're right," I said to her. "Let's forget about everything else and focus only on Draven."

"Your dad bested Draven," Rook said, "in the Great Hall of Strong Haven Palace, when he used his magic to enter his body and immobilize him."

"You beat him too," Uncle Manny said to me. "Back in the bakery, when you unleashed your power and expelled him from the building. You even brought *Abuela* back from death."

Lady Sonia considered me with a raised brow. "You did that, Lady Gabriela?"

I shrugged. "I did, but I have no idea what I did or how I did it. So I don't think I could even repeat it if I tried."

"If you did it once, you can do it again," Rook said. "It is the law of all things."

"Absolutely," Uncle Manny said.

"Maybe," I muttered.

Lady Sonia stayed focused on me. "Your innate power is the rarest and most natural I have ever seen. It is quite remarkable."

"Thank you, Lady Sonia. I get it from my Avila side of the family, and even my Rodriguez side. I'm sure my fae bloodline has something to do with it too."

I thought of her words and latched on to the phrase innate power. I continued poking the stick around the dirt and leaves, thinking of the energy shift I had felt when I was with Leaf and Draven walked in.

Lifting my gaze from the ground, I asked, "If I get my power from my dad's side of the family, then where does Draven get his power?"

Lady Sonia smoothed out the skirt of her dress. "Draven is complicated. Some say he was simply born with an evil spirit in him. He is fae, but also a soul slayer."

"Wait a minute, you called him a soul slayer. Don't you mean soul vamp?" I asked.

"A soul vamp, a soul slayer. There are many different names for what Draven the Witch is. Names that have evolved over the years," Lady Sonia explained.

"That is true," Rook tacked on. "Many different titles, but all with the same meaning. Draven is a villainous murderer who sucks souls from people, and the souls give him strength."

All the lessons my parents and Uncle Leto taught me over the years swirled in my head as I tried to make sense of who Draven was and what kind of power he wielded.

"Fae are ruthless, vengeful, and manipulative," I said, repeating what they taught me. "They cannot lie, but do not need to because they are cunning and devious. They are immortal, but not impervious to being killed. They are incredibly strong, but fall down to iron. Above all else, knowing your enemy can mean the difference between life and death."

"Those are Leto's words," Uncle Manny said. "I remember them well."

We locked eyes, both of us knowing those words could help us. Analyzing each phrase, I focused on one. "Know your enemy," I said slowly, rising to my feet. "It's the most important lesson."

"That's right," Uncle Manny added, with an edge of hope in his voice.

I didn't even realize Lady Sonia had risen to her feet and was standing in front of me. "Follow your intuition," she encouraged me. "What is it telling you?"

Goose bumps erupted all over me as I suddenly thought of the book I had found back in Strong Haven

Palace. I dropped my stick. "I know Draven. Really and truly know him, because I read about him." I shook my head because what I wanted to say wasn't coming out right. "I mean, I read about the very first soul vamp."

Lady Sonia stepped back, stunned. "You did? Where?"

"I was in the library by my room, back at the palace, before everything got crazy. I wanted to know more about Faevenly and found a book that looked interesting. It ended up being the story of the first soul vamp, a witch named Keres."

"Keres?" Lady Sonia asked. "Are you sure?"

I nodded. "Absolutely sure."

"That's great!" Uncle Manny said, slapping his hands together. "The book must have clues about how we can defeat Draven. We may have a chance after all! Did you read the whole story? Do you remember it?"

"The book was really thick, and there was a lot to it, so no. I didn't read it all."

"What did you read, then?" Rook asked.

"Well, this Keres witch was wounded in some sort of battle and needed blood to survive. Her witch sisters took her to a magical forest, where they killed a unicorn. They gave Keres the blood, but it turned out the unicorn wasn't a unicorn, but some sort of demonic shapeshifter. When Keres woke up, she was a soul vamp."

"Whoa," Uncle Manny said. "So that's how the whole soul vamp thing started?"

"Gabriela, this is important," Lady Sonia said. She

leaned forward and spoke in one of those ultra-serious tones. "The story of Keres and her witch family is legendary. Over the course of time, their tale has been exaggerated, changed, and modified in many different ways. There is only one true written account of them, but most believe it is lost. Do you know where that book is?"

"I'm pretty sure I left it in my room back at the palace."

"The palace?" Uncle Manny asked with a gulp. "Where Draven is?"

Lady Sonia looked at Rook with a raised brow, then at me and Uncle Manny.

Manny pinched the bridge of his nose. "Sonia, please don't say what I think you're about to say."

"I am sorry, Manny. But I am going to say it." She looked at each of us in turn, but rested her final stare on me. "We have to go back to the palace and get that book."

"Go back?" I uttered.

Lady Sonia, Rook, and Manny launched into a heated discussion on the dangers associated with going back, while I withdrew inside my own thoughts.

My stomach clenched at the idea of a deadly face-off with Draven, but then another thought occurred to me. If we had the book, we could use it to find those witches. If they were the first soul vamps, and Draven was one of them, they had to have information to help us—information that wasn't written down.

"You're right, Sonia," I said softly, my words

silencing their debate. "I know it'll be dangerous, but we need to get that book and use it to find those witches and ask them for help."

"What?" Uncle Manny said.

Breathing in a deep breath, I said, "We go to the palace and get that book so we can find those witches. I feel like they're the answer." But then my mind filled with Leaf. The image of him alone in that dungeon, injured and helpless, had broken me. If I could help him, I had to try. He meant too much to me not to. "We can also rescue Leaf."

"What? Absolutely not!" Uncle Manny countered with emotion. "I'm not even addressing how horrible an idea it is to search for a group of soul sucking witches. But now you want to rescue Leaf? He betrayed us. And because of him, a lot of people were killed. Including your mom!"

I blinked away the tears that bubbled to the surface, not wanting to respond with emotion. There was no time for that. But I had to make my uncle understand. "He was made to do it, Uncle Manny. He told me. We can't turn our backs on him just because Draven used him. I mean, if something like that happened to you, wouldn't you want us to come for you?"

Uncle Manny wagged his finger at me. "Come on, that's not a fair example."

Lady Sonia chimed in. "It is a sound idea. We go for the book, rescue Leaf, and then use the book to find the soul witches. They will have valuable information."

Rook worked his jaw, and he didn't even have to say anything for me to know what he was thinking. He and Leaf were close. "I am in agreement."

A crunching of leaves stopped our discussion. I sucked in a breath, then searched around for my fighting stick, but it was over by my pallet. Making do with what was nearby, I snatched up a rock and gripped it tight. Manny raised the cup he still held. Rook drew his dagger.

"It is Adrius and Verona!" Adrius called out.

The horses trotted into view, carrying Adrius and Verona, dressed in the same copper clothes they'd worn earlier. Their long dark hair was braided tightly behind their backs, and their horses were loaded with bags and weapons.

Rook raised his brows in surprise and lowered his dagger. "What are you two doing here?"

Adrius brought his horse to a stop and hopped down. "We are here to offer our assistance, Lord Rook."

"You are?" Rook asked, switching his gaze to Verona.

She hopped off her horse too. "Not to the daughter of Strong Haven, but to you. Our brother Sublander. We are here for you."

"Okayyy," I whispered to myself.

"What of the Sublands council?" Lady Sonia asked, glossing over the *not to the daughter of Strong Haven* part. "What do they say about you two leaving?"

"We did not consult with them," Adrius replied, "though I am sure they have discovered our absence by now. We are willing to face those consequences later."

"The council does not control us," Verona added defiantly. "Not now, not ever. And while I will never bow to a Strong, I owe you my allegiance, Rook."

Really? Without even thinking, I marched up to her. She towered over my petite frame, but I didn't let that intimidate me. I was a Strong princess and an Avila *bruja*.

"I'm not asking you to bow to me because I don't need you to bow to me. Not now, not ever," I said, throwing her words back at her. "Got it?"

Verona crossed her arms in front of her, considering me for a few seconds before glancing at Rook.

"Back away, Verona," Rook warned.

Manny pulled me back and eased me away from Verona. "Let's not do this, ladies," he said to me and her. "Okay? I mean, we're on the same side, right?"

Neither one of us replied to Manny, but like boxers in a match, we retreated to opposite ends of the camp.

Rook moved closer to the fire, as if he were a general about to make a speech. "Verona and Adrius, I am most pleased to have you join us, but there are things you should know and assurances you must make. First and foremost, to support me means to support Lady Gabriela. We are aligned in our mission. Do you accept that?"

"Yes," Adrius answered.

Verona shifted her stance before saying, "Yes."

Rook grunted his approval, then went on. "Our

mission is fraught with danger, and there is a strong possibility some of us will be killed. Only last night, we were attacked by two assassins at the manor. If not for the warnings we received, we could have perished. Do you accept the dangers of our mission?"

"Of course," Adrius answered.

"You know I accept the danger," Verona huffed. "There is no issue there. But who sent the assassins?"

Rook's eyes narrowed, his anger over our attack resurfacing. "Draven, no doubt, but with Lord Kane's hand."

"Lord Kane?" I asked, shocked because Rook hadn't mentioned that. "How do you know?"

"There was no time for me to mention it sooner, but I am sure I saw one of the assassins with Lord Kane of High Meadow when we were at the meeting of the Council of Six."

"The Kanes?" Uncle Manny said. "No surprise there, I guess. Alexander was killed, after all."

"True," I muttered.

"But the Kanes are not our priority," Rook pointed out. "Draven is. So let us focus on that as we strategize."

As glad as I was to have reinforcements, I wasn't crazy about it being Verona and her brother. Not that I minded her brother, but Verona's hatred for me came off her in waves like a thick fog. But I had to believe that if they stood with Rook, and Rook stood with me, then I could trust them.

Right?

12

GABRIELA

Lady Sonia set fresh logs on the dying campfire, then stoked the embers with a long stick. The flames rejuvenated, springing to life and sending sparks and pops into the cool forest air. Verona and Adrius stayed close together, sitting on one side of the flames, while Rook and the rest of us sat together on the other side.

"Lord Rook, before we discuss the plans you all have and how we may be of assistance," Adrius said, "you should know that Lord Leto and his caravan arrived at the Sublands."

"Did the Sublands turn him away?" Rook asked with an angry undertone.

"Lord Leto and his guards, yes. They head to the manor in the west. But the citizens of Strong Haven, no. They are safe in the city."

Manny clutched my knee and whispered, "Thank you, Jesus. Draven doesn't have them."

Verona whipped her stare at him. "Why would Draven the Witch have them?"

"Because he has Strong Haven East," I answered for my uncle. "And Leaf."

"Draven has Leaf?" Verona's expression hardened, all emotion draining away as she straightened.

"Thunderation," Adrius added quickly. "Draven has Strong Haven East *and* Leaf? Are you sure?"

"Yes," Rook answered with a nod. "We are sure."

"We must get Leaf immediately," Verona declared, jumping to her feet, ready to charge to the palace on foot.

I tilted my head, surprised at her reaction, but then reminded myself that if she and Adrius were close to Rook, then they were probably close to Leaf too.

"Well, that's one thing we agree on," I said to her.

She swiveled her head my way. "You wish to rescue Leaf?"

"Yes, I do. He's very important to me."

If her look was hateful before, it was murderous now. Her violet eyes narrowed, and her nostrils flared. I didn't respond to her at all and kept my exterior cool even though inside I was stunned.

Did she have a thing for Leaf?

"Enough, Verona," Rook said in an exasperated tone as he rubbed his temples. "Sit. Please."

Verona lowered herself to her seat. But I didn't have to look at her to feel the heat from her glare. I kept my head up and my attention on Rook, refusing to give her the satisfaction of intimidating me, but also burning to know if there was something between her and Leaf.

"Rescuing Leaf is only part of our plan," Rook went on. "The other part of the plan involves retrieving a book from Lady Gabriela's chambers."

Adrius perked up. "A book? What kind of book?"

"A book that has information about Draven," I answered, wondering if he caught on to the dagger-filled stares Verona was shooting at me. If he did, he gave no clue. Or maybe he didn't notice because they were siblings and he was used to it.

A gurgling sound came from Uncle Manny. He slammed his hands over his stomach then said in a sheepish voice, "Oh, my gosh. Sorry, y'all." The grumble repeated, this time even louder. "Um." He stood carefully. "I think nature is calling. Excuse me."

He casually but quickly weaved his way out of the campfire circle and disappeared into the woods.

"Nature is calling?" Adrius asked, peering about. "I do not hear anything."

"It's an expression," I explained. "It means he needs to use the bathroom."

"Oh," Adrius replied, still looking a little confused.

I flashed Lady Sonia a look. "The potion, maybe?"

"Perhaps," she muttered, looking in the direction where Manny had gone. "I may have been too generous with some of the ingredients."

With Uncle Manny gone, the group went back to the matter at hand. "What were we saying?" Rook asked.

"We were discussing going to the Strong Haven East Palace to find a book and rescue Leaf," Verona said. "A plan I wholeheartedly support. But we cannot all go. Six is too many if we want to remain undetected.

I propose only the most skilled will go. Me, Adrius, Lord Rook, and Lady Sonia."

Excuse me? She wanted to leave me and Uncle Manny behind? She had no idea what I was capable of, and her disregard for me was really beginning to piss me off.

"I don't think so," I said to Verona, giving her my full attention. "And let me make this conversation a whole lot easier for you. Strong Haven is my home. I am the heir to the throne. And that book we are looking for belongs to me. So I'm going, and so is my uncle, Rook, and Lady Sonia. You two are the ones who aren't needed."

Verona raised her brow and considered me for a few seconds. "You are a fool if you think you do not need me and Adrius. After Rook we are the next strongest fighters in this group."

"Did you just call me a fool?" I spat, hands curled into fists at my sides and brows furrowed as I rose to my feet.

"Enough!" Rook called out in an exasperated tone. "We all go, and that is final!"

"Wise idea," Lady Sonia offered before anyone could say anything else. I lowered myself back down and drew in a deep breath. "We all go, and we use the tunnels to get us to the palace undetected."

Adrius scooted in, as if Lady Sonia had just spilled an ancient secret. Even Verona's attitude was cooled off by her words.

"The tunnels?" Adrius asked. "I have heard rumors of them. Do they really exist?"

"Tunnels?" I asked.

Verona smirked. "It is your home. You do not know of your own tunnels?"

"Verona," Rook hissed.

Lady Sonia cleared her throat, as if clearing the air. "There is a system of tunnels beneath Strong Haven Palace and Strong Haven Manor. Many consider them to be myth because they are never talked about. There are several entry points and exit points, and I know where each one is."

"Excellent," Rook announced. "Thank you, Lady Sonia. Now we only need to decide when to go. And how. Time is of the essence, and unfortunately the horses we have been riding are too slow for what we need."

Lady Sonia rubbed her chin. "The only beast I know that is fast enough and will allow riders is the Enbarr. Though I do not know how to summon them."

Rook grunted in frustration. "I do not either. But we must find a way. We need their swift transport."

"I have heard others summon them," Adrius offered. "Perhaps I can replicate the sound."

A piercing scream shot through the air, the kind that silenced you with a shudder and made your heart stop beating.

Uncle Manny!

I shot to my feet, ran to my pallet, and grabbed my fighting stick, then raced the way Uncle Manny had gone. I didn't have to go too far before I saw him on the ground, curled up on his side, clutching his stomach.

"Uncle Manny!" I crashed down next to him, my heart in my throat as he writhed in pain, his face so pale he didn't even look like himself.

"S-s-something is w-w-wrong with me," he panted.

Sweat beads covered his forehead, and a green tint colored his lips. I turned and yelled, "Lady Sonia!"

"I am here!" She crouched down next to me with her bag in her arms and touched Manny's forehead. "He is ice cold," she muttered. She moved in close. "Manny, did you use the bathroom?"

He groaned deep and shook his head, his eyes closed tight. "No. D-d-didn't have t-t-too."

She rifled through her things, then brought out her vial of green liquid from the healing water... and there wasn't that much.

"Oh, no," I muttered under my breath, eyeing the half-empty vial.

"It will be enough," she assured me. She held Manny's head up with one hand and the vial with the other. "I am going to give you a liquid that you need to swallow."

With his entire body trembling, he managed a weak nod.

She pressed the glass to his parted lips, and poured slowly. He sipped the drops in intervals, taking his time to get the liquid down. When he finished, she lowered his head carefully. His contorted face eased some and his ragged breathing slowed to almost normal.

Rook crouched on the other side of us. "Should I move him to his pallet?"

Before Lady Sonia could answer, Manny uttered with chattering teeth, "Y-y-yess. C-c-cold."

With a nod to me and Lady Sonia, Rook slid his arms under Uncle Manny and lifted his small frame with ease. He carried him back to the campfire where our things were and set him down on the pallet he had slept on the night before. Adrius tapped me on the shoulder and handed me a blanket. I took it with a thanks, then covered Uncle Manny, tucking in the sides. His brow smoothed out and his head lolled to the side as he fell asleep. I watched my sweet uncle for a while, not even realizing I was holding my breath until I let it out.

"Is he going to be okay?" I asked out loud, not exactly knowing where Lady Sonia was but feeling her presence nearby.

She came around in front of me and said, "Yes. He will be."

Studying my uncle, it looked like he was simply taking a nice, hard nap. There were no signs at all of his feeling sick. No sweat on his forehead, no green lips, no trembling. Even his tan color had returned to his face.

"What happened to him?" I asked her.

She shook her head slowly. "I can only guess he had a reaction to one of the ingredients in my potion. For that, I am deeply sorry, Princess. But with that dose of pure green healing water, he should be fine when he awakes. I do hope you will forgive me."

"Of course I forgive you. It was an accident. Besides, he's okay now," I said, grabbing her arm and giving her a squeeze.

"Thank you, Princess."

I stayed by Uncle Manny's side the rest of the day. I checked his forehead in intervals, adjusted his blanket every time he shifted, and took his pulse to make sure his heart was beating strong. Lady Sonia joined in too, assessing him periodically and assuring me he was okay.

When the sun dipped down and the sky turned dark, everyone settled in for the night. Nudging my pallet over, I moved as close as I could to my uncle. Even Rook and Lady Sonia seemed to do the same as the four of us stayed near one another as we slept. I had no idea where Verona and Adrius were sleeping, and I didn't care. They were the least of my problems.

I rolled onto my side so I could watch my uncle, the faint rise and fall of his chest the only thing keeping me steady. My fingers found the cross at my neck, the metal cool against my skin, grounding me in the moment. I prayed for him to be okay. I couldn't take losing another loved one.

13

GABRIELA

Somewhere between worrying about Uncle Manny, my parents, and Leaf, I fell asleep. It was the kind of slumber that was shallow and restless and filled with the most bizarre dreams—me at home with my parents eating a dinner of dirt and worms; me at the coffee shop with my cousin Aliana when a tornado came through and swept us away, and finally me with Leaf on a sinking boat filled with baby ducks.

The ducks were excited about the rising water, while I was terrified. I scrambled to scoop the water out with cupped hands while Leaf kept telling me everything was going to be okay. When the water covered my nose and I was seconds away from drowning, my eyes flung open. I stayed perfectly still, hand on my chest, the pale blue morning sky telling me I wasn't in that boat after all but in the woods of Faevenly.

"I'm okay," I whispered to myself, slowing my breathing. "Everything is okay."

I peered at my Uncle Manny and saw that he was sleeping peacefully on his stomach with his blanket pulled up high and only tufts of hair showing. After watching his steady rhythmic breathing for a while, I got up and went into the woods for a few minutes, then returned back to camp.

Rook bustled about the fire, setting fresh logs on our remaining embers and tossing in clumps of brush and leaves. The fire caught on quickly and the flames sparked and popped with new life.

I yawned, then rubbed my face. "Where are Lady Sonia and the others?"

"They are foraging for breakfast," he said, poking the fire. "They should be returning soon."

I yawned again, even bigger than before, the kind of yawn that made your whole body shake.

"You should get more sleep. Today promises to be a big day, and it would be wise to be well rested."

"You're probably right," I said, scratching my head. "I'll go lie down for a bit more."

I was starting back for my spot when it dawned on me that I was alone with Rook. Completely and totally alone. With the others gone, I could ask him about Verona and fish for information about her and Leaf. I wanted to know if there was something between them. I also wanted to know if I could trust her.

"Hey, Rook. Can I ask you something?"

"Of course, my lady." He dropped the remaining sticks on the fire, then dusted his hands and came over to me. "What is on your mind?"

"Well," I said, trying to figure out the right words for what I wanted to say. "I wanted to know a little more about Verona, I mean, besides her hating me because I'm a Strong."

"Verona," he muttered. "What can I say? She is strong and confident, but also volatile and impetuous. She makes no secret of her thoughts and feelings, like the ones she has already expressed about the Strong name. But despite that, she is a loyal friend. She always does what is right. I know that no matter what, I can count on her. And she can count on me."

"I see," I muttered. "So that means I can count on her too?"

"Without a doubt," he assured. "She is with me, and you are with me. She would never go against that."

I wanted to ask about Leaf, but struggled with the right words because I didn't want to sound petty or insecure or prying. "What about Leaf? Are they… close?"

Rook's eyes softened, as if understanding what I was getting at. "They are, but not in the same way that he is close with you."

A wave of relief came over me, but I didn't let it show. "Thanks, Rook."

Back on my pallet, I snuggled under my blanket as best as I could on my side and folded my hands under my head. I watched the slight movement of Uncle Manny's back as he breathed in and breathed out. He was a huge part of my life and had done so much for me and my family. If anything happened to him, I didn't know what I'd do.

Thinking about how important he was brought on

a wave of homesickness. I missed my parents, my home, my lake, and my *abuela*. I hadn't tried to contact her with my mind because when Uncle Manny and I left the human realm, she was still in the hospital. I prayed she was okay.

A soft moan came from my uncle, followed by a yawn. After that, he stretched. I sat up, relieved for him to be waking.

"Hey, you feeling okay?"

He stretched again, this time letting out a satisfied grunt. "Better than ever, *mija*."

He flipped from his stomach to his back and turned around to face me. My eyes widened. My mouth dropped. I didn't even understand what I was looking before a scream shot out of me.

Uncle Manny sat up in a panic. "*Mija*, what is it?"

I jumped to my feet and slammed my hands over my mouth in disbelief. He jumped to his feet too. "What?" he asked in a yell.

Rook raced over to us, dagger in hand, but lowered it as soon as he neared. He looked at Manny, then at me, then back to Manny.

"Manny?" he asked.

Uncle Manny's brows raised and his lips parted. "*¿Qué es?* Did that potion do something to me?" He brought his hands to his face and patted all around his cheeks and forehead. "Am I hideous?" He held his hands out in front of him and studied both sides carefully. "What in the holy hell?" He brought his hands to his face again.

"Why does my face feel smooth and my hands look young?"

Inching closer to him and studying him from head to toe with my eyes practically bulging out of my head and my heart racing, I uttered, "They look young because... they *are* young. I mean, you. You are young."

He gaped. "I'm... young?"

Goose bumps erupted all over my body as I grappled with what I was looking at, not even understanding what had happened to my uncle. "Yeah, really young. Like, my age."

Rook narrowed his stare and studied Manny as if examining a foreign object. "Incredible. You look the way you did when you were last in Faevenly so many years ago. But with shorter hair."

Manny moved his hands to his neck, then his chest, patting and prodding. He glanced down at his pants that hung a little loose. Then he slapped himself. "Am I dreaming?" He slapped himself again.

I grabbed his hand to stop him from another whack, then poked his cheek with my other hand. "You're definitely not dreaming."

Lady Sonia, Verona, and Adrius walked into camp with armfuls of berries and apples and fresh wood. They stopped dead in their tracks when they spotted Manny, their expressions mirroring ours.

"Sun, moon, and stars," Lady Sonia uttered. "Manny?" She lowered her things to the ground in slow motion, then walked over to him.

He met her halfway, his eyes bright, and his face

youthful and fresh. "I, uh, think your potion did something to me."

"It appears so." She held her hands up to his face. "May I?"

"Yeah, sure."

She touched his forehead, then closed her eyes. Her lips moved as if she was saying something, but I couldn't hear anything. She moved her hands down to his temples and kept them there for a while before resting them on his shoulders.

She opened her eyes, dropped her hands, and stepped back. "It was not what I had intended, but it seems I reversed your aging all the way to this age that you are now. My apologies."

"Apologies? Are you kidding me?" He rubbed his lower back, his mouth hanging open in disbelief. "All my aches and pains are gone. It's like one big giant, witchy do-over."

He had no wrinkles at all, no sign of weariness around his eyes, no sprinkle of gray hair at his temples. It was like he'd taken a drink from the fountain of youth. Which, I guess he kinda had.

"This is incredible, Lady Sonia," Rook said, circling Manny as if he were an object to observe and not a person. "Are you able to replicate the potion?"

She placed her long elegant fingers on her chin. "I do not know. I improvised with many of the ingredients and did not have exact measurements. But I suppose I could try. I did concoct a potion for Lady Celyse to allow her to age at the same rate as Julio when she was in the human realm. What I concocted for Manny, it appears, is the extreme version of that."

"It is worth looking into later," Rook said. "Although fae age at a much slower rate than humans, a potion that can reverse aging would be most beneficial."

"For the humans who live here especially," Lady Sonia said with a nod at Rook. "Perhaps I can work on that later."

Uncle Manny held up his hand and let out a nervous laugh. "Um, hello? Can we hold on a second here?"

"Of course, Manny," Lady Sonia said, turning her attention away from Rook and back on my uncle.

With everyone staring at him, I could tell he didn't know what to say. So instead, he slammed his hand on mine and pulled me with him. "I need to talk to Gabriela. We'll be right back."

He walked at a quick pace, weaving in and out of the trees. When he got far enough away from the others, he stopped and released my hand and turned to face me.

His mouth fell open and he stayed like that for a while. "Is this really happening?"

"It's happening, or, uh, it happened." I had seen pictures of my dad and Uncle Manny when they were young, so I knew what that version of him looked like. But seeing Manny's younger self in front of me, in the flesh, had me stunned.

He walked around in a small circle, staring down at

his legs, as if testing everything out. "*Dios mío*. I can't even believe it," he muttered. "I mean, what the hell?"

I stifled a chuckle as I kept a keen eye on him. "And you feel totally fine?"

"More than fine," he answered as he jumped up and down. And then he did a backflip. "*Mija!* I haven't been able to do that since college!"

"Uncle Manny," I laughed. "Don't overdo it."

He did another flip, ignoring me, and landed with a huge smile. "You know what else is weird? I feel mentally like my eighteen-year-old self." He tapped the side of his head. "I don't feel like a forty-year-old dude up here."

"Um, I can see that."

He came over to me with a serious expression. "But that doesn't mean anything has changed. I'm still your elder and you still have to listen to me."

I raised a brow, but instead of saying something snarky, I agreed with him. "I know, Uncle Manny. Nothing has changed at all, besides the way you look."

"That's right," he nodded.

I kept staring at him, still in awe over his new self, but forced myself to push all that away. "So I guess we keep on like nothing happened?"

He shrugged. "We have to."

I drew in a deep breath and blew it out fast. "Well, let's return to the others and figure out how to get all the way back to the palace for the book, and for Leaf... without getting killed."

He gulped. "Yeah, that would really suck if I had this new self and then got killed."

We weaved our way back the way we had come, my mind still processing Uncle Manny's new body but also focused on the not-getting-killed part, because he was right.

That would really suck.

14

GABRIELA

ady Sonia, Rook, Verona, and Adrius were standing close together and separated when they saw us approaching. Lady Sonia came our way, wearing a look of concern.

"Is all well?" she asked Manny. "Other than, of course, your new youthfulness?"

He rubbed the back of his neck. "I guess so, all things considered."

"Good," Rook said. "Then let us get back to the matter at hand. We must find a way to return to Strong Haven Palace as soon as possible. We were discussing the idea of using the Enbarr."

"Yeah, that's right," I muttered, our conversation from earlier coming back to me.

"Enbarr?" Manny asked with a gulp. "Those really tall and really fast horses?"

"You've been on one, Uncle Manny?"

"Yeah, I have. Leto summoned them and we made it from his cottage to Strong Haven Palace in hours as opposed to days. Riding them was like being on a high-speed train... with no windows."

"The only problem is we do not know how to summon them," Lady Sonia said.

Adrius chimed in. "I have seen others summon Enbarr. Since you have too, Manny, perhaps we can work together on replicating the call."

"Yeah, sure," Manny shrugged. "We can try."

"It is settled, then," Rook said, clapping his hands together. "Adrius and Manny will work on summoning the Enbarr while the rest of us pack up our things."

Keeping one eye on Manny, I rolled up my sleeping pallet as well as his, not even believing we were the same age. Tucking those aside, I got busy folding our blankets, wondering what I should call him—Uncle Manny or just Manny? Not that his newfound youth changed that he was still my dad's best friend and my uncle. Or did it? Would he now be my friend? I shuddered, thinking talking to him like a friend would be so weird, and so wrong.

I glanced his way again. He and Adrius were busy whistling. They tried low, then high, and all kinds of different pitches in between. They cupped their hands around their mouths, they even whistled in unison. They laughed, as if having a good time, and I marveled at the magic of it all.

Young Manny... such a strange concept.

With mine and Manny's stuff gathered up, I got busy shoving everything into our bags that hung over the saddle blankets. I stopped and admired the steeds and their beauty. What would happen to the regular horses once the Enbarr showed up? *If* the Enbarr showed up.

Lady Sonia must have sensed my thoughts somehow. "Are you thinking about what will become of these creatures when we leave them?"

"Actually, yes," I nodded. "Where will they go?"

Lady Sonia patted the horse's neck and smiled, giving it a few long strokes. "They know where their home is. They will return there." She gave me a reassuring smile. "You need not fear."

Lady Sonia went back to her tasks while I stayed by the horses, watching everything around me. Manny and Adrius were still working together on calling the Enbarr, Lady Sonia was packing up her bag of herbs and oils and things, and Rook was stamping out the fire and cleaning up the cooking stuff.

Continuing with my casual scan, my gaze landed on Verona. She sat on a stump, looking me up and down, shooting daggers with her eyes. Even though I wanted to turn away, I felt like I couldn't. As if doing so would make her better than me, or give her some sort of power. So I held steady.

Rook had said she and Leaf were close, but not as close as he was with me. But now, with her glare on me, I wondered exactly what he meant, and regretted not asking. But did I really need to know? She had to have been in love with Leaf. There was no other explanation for her hostility toward me. I wondered what Leaf thought of her. If he even knew how she felt. Or maybe they had a thing, but it was long over.

I moved over to her and sat on a nearby log. I cleared my throat. "I have no idea what I did to you, but whatever it is, I'm really hoping we can get past it."

She crossed her arms and straightened her back. "You would do well enough to leave it alone."

I crossed my arms, mirroring her, and sat a little taller. "It would be a lot easier for me to leave *it* alone if you tell me what *it* is."

She narrowed her eyes. "*It* is my years of friendship with Leaf. *It* is the closeness I have shared with him. I was there long before you." Her gaze hardened. "Just because you have shown up with a title to your name does not make you better than me. Or anyone else."

I sat back, a little stunned. "I certainly don't think I'm better than you or anyone else. And I know full well that you and Leaf have been friends for a long time. But he and I are close too. The sooner you come to terms with that, the better for all of us."

She leaned forward. "Do not ever tell me what to do."

I let out an exasperated sigh and rose to my feet. "You know what? Forget it. You do you, and I'll do me."

I went back to fiddling with my horse, and was moving around items in the saddlebags when I heard the sound of a flute. I looked over my shoulder and saw Uncle Manny and Adrius looking somewhat wide-eyed. I joined them quickly.

"Did that sound come from y'all?"

"Yes," Uncle Manny said with a grin, smacking

Adrius on the back. "From Adrius. And I'm certain that was the same whistle that Leto used."

"I am certain as well that it was the correct call," Adrius added with a smile.

Rook, Lady Sonia, and Verona gathered around and Rook clapped Adrius on the back. "Good work. Now let us see if they come."

My hope dashed away because I thought calling them was a sure thing. "Do they sometimes not come?"

"It depends," Lady Sonia answered. "They are emotional and temperamental creatures and only do what they want to do. So if they want to answer the call, they will. If they do not, they will not. Either way, we will know soon."

"Let's hope they're in the mood, then," I muttered.

I stayed close to Manny, waiting for a sound like a train or a hard gallop, feeling a little bit scared of what might come, but nothing happened. Seconds ticked by, then minutes. I was beginning to think we were out of luck.

"How long do we wait?" I asked in a half whisper.

"Shhh," Lady Sonia said, so low I barely heard her. "Listen."

A light wind swept through the woods, rustling the leaves in waves. The breeze sent down a sprinkle of branches and leaves and a pine cone thudded near my boot. As if delighted by the gust, our horses gathered together and started stamping and nickering.

"They are coming," Lady Sonia whispered.

"They are?" Hope swelled inside of me, along with

excitement. How would they show themselves? Would they charge in like a cavalry? Or swoop in from above like a Pegasus? I glanced up at the trees just in case, expecting a huge spectacle, when four magnificent and tall white horses strolled into the clearing.

They made no sound at all, as if their hooves were magically enhanced with some sort of whispering stealth mode. They were taller than tall, like an elk or a moose. But also slender, with no bulk at all. Their white coats glistened with a pearlized sheen, and their manes hung long and flowy.

They studied us with purple eyes amidst long white lashes, their gazes curious and interested. Even their snouts twitched with inquisitiveness.

"Incredible," I uttered, almost holding my breath.

"They really are," Uncle Manny said.

One of the Enbarr approached Adrius and nudged him playfully on the shoulder. Adrius smiled and stroked it between the eyes. "Hello, beautiful Enbarr."

"It recognizes you as the one who sent the call," Lady Sonia said.

Adrius kept stroking the steed. "So smart. Thank you for answering." It snorted, and the others snorted too, and I wondered if they were all linked. "We are seeking passage to the Strong Haven Palace in the East. Will you provide it?"

The Enbarr reached out one of its hooves and stamped it on the ground with a low whinny.

"That looks like a yes," I said with a dazzled smile.

"Most definitely a yes," Lady Sonia confirmed.

"Thank you very much," Adrius said.

Rook pulled everyone away from the wonder of the Enbarr by pointing at things and issuing orders in his usual gruff demeanor and husky voice. "We ride light. Weapons only. Pack up everything else. Secure whatever is not needed to the horses to be sent back to Strong Haven Manor. We leave at once."

Uncle Manny nudged up beside me and patted my back. "You okay with getting on the Enbarr, *mija*?"

"Yeah, sure," I said, staring at him and studying his smooth skin and brown hair, thinking him calling me *mija* sounded so weird now. "So... do I still call you Uncle Manny?"

He blinked. "Of course! I'm still your uncle, you know, and I always will be. No matter how young I look."

Rook came by us, still gathering things and getting organized, and shot us a look.

"Um, let's finish getting our stuff," Uncle Manny said.

Adrius and Verona strapped on their bows and quivers, along with their fighting sticks and daggers. I took my fighting stick and slung it on my back too. Manny had taken off his belt with his dagger, but buckled it back around his waist. Lady Sonia never showed her weapon, but I knew it was secured under her dress. She also had her bag with her potions and things on her back like a backpack.

With the manor horses loaded up with the stuff we didn't need, Rook patted one and said, "Go on. Go home. Back to the manor."

The horse started trotting away, and the others followed. They seemed to bow their heads as they passed by the Enbarr, then took off in an easy gallop when they entered the trees.

Rook and the others walked up to our new rides. With four of them and six of us, two of us would need to share. Rook was quick to make the first suggestion. "Lady Gabriela will go with me."

I had no problem with that arrangement. Rook was strong, and knowing I'd be riding a supersonic magical horse with him made me feel easier about the whole thing.

"Thanks, Rook," I said.

"Adrius and I will ride together," Verona volunteered.

"I guess that means you and I get our own rides," Uncle Manny said to Lady Sonia, not looking at all excited about being alone on the fast beast.

With the riding arrangements set, Adrius and Verona leapt onto their horses like graceful acrobats. Even with a dress on, Lady Sonia had no problem getting on her ride either. Uncle Manny and I, on the other hand, needed boosts from Rook.

Once we were all in place, and before we took off, Lady Sonia let out a small gasp. Her hand went to the opal necklace that hung around her neck.

Rook eyed her with a frown. "What is it, Lady Sonia?"

She scanned the woods and even the skies, as if searching for something. "I am not sure. But I feel something is amiss in Faevenly."

"Something more than what's already happening?" I asked. "Like what?"

She lowered her hand, and I thought I detected a slight tremble in her fingers. "I know not."

"Whatever it is," Rook said, "I am sure we will find out soon enough." He secured his fighting stick in front of him, then reached out and stroked the Enbarr's coat. "Take us to the outer edges of Strong Haven Palace. To the shadows."

The Enbarr didn't move. Instead, it stamped its hooves. "I think I need to ask," Adrius said.

"Well, go ahead, then," Rook said with irritation.

"Magnificent Enbarr," Adrius said, "please take us to the outer edges of Strong Haven Palace. To the shadows."

With a huff, the Enbarr walked out of the clearing as quietly as they had entered, their hooves making no sound at all. Their tall and lean bodies seemed to glide over the earth with each stride, and every movement smooth and effortless. With each forward motion, their pace quickened, and soon the grass and brush and trees blurred. The wind whipped against my face and shut my eyes. I tightened my arms around Rook's waist and buried myself against his back.

As we raced across Faevenly, I didn't care about the dangers of the high-speed. My mind stayed on Leaf. Lady Sonia had felt something was off, and for some reason I thought it had to do with him.

Please still be alive.

15

LEAF

My eyes opened. First one, and then the other. But not by my own effort. Some was peeling back my eyelids. The outline of a tiny creature came into view—ridged tree-bark skin, a fluttering of gold, tiny yellow eyes.

"Majestic," I mumbled.

"Lovely Leaf!" the high-pitched sprite cried. "Oh my, oh my, beautiful fae creature. You are in a state. Can you hear me?"

"Yes." I swallowed. "I can hear you."

She twirled and backed up so I could get my bearings. "Are you able to sit up?"

I nodded. "Yes."

Every bone in my body throbbed as I hoisted myself off the ground and leaned against the stone wall. Enough daylight streamed in from above to reveal blood-soaked cuts crisscrossing up and down my clothing. Raising my hands, I could not even see my own skin through the red stains.

Soft sobs came from her tiny lips. "Who did this to you, Lovely Leaf?" Her shoulders shook as she wiped her eyes. "Who?"

"The evil being. He did this to me."

"Who is it? I must know the name of this wretched being!"

I drew in a long breath. "Draven."

She gasped and pressed her delicate hands against her mouth. "Draven Midlothian? The fae witch and soul stealer? Oh my, oh my. That is awful." She zipped back and forth frantically. "I am so frightened! So very frightened!"

I patted the ground. "Sit, Majestic. It is okay. We will hear him if he comes, and you can easily fly away."

She fluttered close, then landed softly on the stone floor. She did not speak, but clasped her hands in front of her. Her eyes were wide with fear.

"What brings you back here?" I asked her.

"I wanted to tell you that I found your lady friend, Gabriela."

A spark of hope lit up inside of me. "You found her?"

"I did. I found her and her group at the Strong Haven Manor in the west. I delivered your message. They were already packing up and leaving."

A sigh of relief seeped from my mouth. "Thank you, Majestic. She will be safe from Draven's assassins, then."

She looked around nervously, as if scared Draven might explode in at any given moment and obliterate us to pieces. I could not blame her and was about to tell her she could leave, when she spoke.

"I am grateful I was able to help. But I am most

frightened, and must go back to my forest now. I do wish you well, Lovely Leaf. I am sorry I could not do more."

"Thank you, Majestic. You did more than you know. I hope our paths meet again, and under more desirable circumstances."

"I hope so too." She fluttered her wings, lifted herself off the ground, then zoomed up and away in a flash.

Leaning my head back, I closed my eyes. Draven could torture me. He could kill me. As long as Gabriela was safe, whatever happened to me did not matter. With my body throbbing and my throat dry like cotton, I closed my eyes.

A creaking sound interrupted my silence and I sat up with a start. Someone had opened the dungeon door and was making their way down the stairs. As I feared, Draven swept into the room, and I braced myself for another visit with my mad captor.

"Here for more?" I gritted out between clenched teeth.

He moved in close, his pale face and sparkling white eyes standing out against his all-black attire. "**Stand.**"

The vibration of his voice worked through, prying me off the floor and pulling me upright. He glided in even closer to me, looking me up and down with satisfaction at having injured me so badly.

"What do you want?" I asked.

He flapped his cloak and stepped back. "What do I

want? Now there is a question I do not mind answering, since while you are under my compulsion, you cannot repeat my answer in any form or fashion. So it gives me great joy to tell you the horrors I plan to unleash horrors you can do nothing about."

I clenched my hands at my sides, wishing I could wrap them around Draven's neck. I imagined all the different ways I would torture him if I could. I was going to find a way to kill him if it was the last thing I did.

"What do you have planned?" I asked.

His wicked smile curled up. "Let me show you. Come."

My legs moved forward, and I followed Draven up the stairs and out of the dungeon. When I emerged into the brightly lit corridor, I shielded my eyes and focused on my blood-stained boots. When my eyes had adjusted well enough, I lowered my hands and saw that we were heading toward the door that led outside.

The day shone bright, and the soft breeze stung my exposed and injured skin. We passed two gardeners tending to a row of azalea bushes. They were short and stocky dwarves, dressed in all green. Their mouths dropped when they saw me, and their shears tumbled out of their hands. One dwarf closed his right hand, placed it over his heart, and made a slight circular motion, signaling his sorrow. But I did not want him to show me any sympathy lest Draven spot it and inflict the same harm on the dwarf. With a slight hand gesture at my side, I waved them away, and the two slipped behind one of the bushes.

We kept walking, moving past the greenery and the fountains and the statues until we reached the area beyond the gardens and to the pathway to Torch Lake. Guards were usually spotted along the gravel road to prevent illegal trespassing and tampering with the shimmers, but today, there were none. A few more steps, and we reached the clearing before the water's edge. I saw there were no guards there either. But then I noticed something else.

The usual haze that hovered over Torch Lake was missing. I narrowed my stare, keeping my eyes fixed on the surface of the lake, wondering why the shimmers would not be casting off their usual mistiness. And when we got to the water's edge, my stomach dropped.

The shimmers were gone.

My blood boiled as the realization hit that Draven had done something to them. "What did you do?" I hissed.

Draven eyed the lake with a wicked stare, then turned his malicious gaze on me. "Humans do not belong in Faevenly," he spat. "Never have. They are an aberration. They are vile, dirty, and inferior. By destroying the portals between our worlds, I am protecting this land."

Terror worked its way through me. If Draven hated humans so much he would destroy the shimmers, what would he do to those living in Faevenly with human blood? I did not care about myself, but what would happen to Gabriela? Even Rook?

Draven moved in closer with a sinister scowl. "With the shimmers gone, my next move will be ending every trace of human blood in Faevenly using the waterways as my vehicle and the aquoise as my weapon. Only then can this realm be fully restored. My mission will begin with Gabriela and the foul human she brought with her from the lesser realm. They will serve as symbols of my new order. As for you, Leaf, you will be my last kill."

I matched his stare as hatred for him flooded me. "Your mission will fail, Draven. I do not know how, but I know it will. As for Princess Gabriela, she has a team of guards protecting her day and night. Some of the strongest in all of Faevenly," I said, knowing full well she had received my warning about the assassins coming for her at the manor, but holding my tongue so he would not discover my knowledge.

He let out a wicked laugh. "I have no doubt I will succeed, in all things. As for the daughter of Strong Haven, I have many assassins, near and far, some dispatched, some waiting for my orders. So it matters not who is guarding her. Especially since no one can match my ultimate assassin, who has not even yet been put into play."

My mind thought of the strongest warriors in Faevenly, wondering who could be working with the vicious witch as an assassin, but having a hard time imagining anyone would have stooped so low to align with Draven.

"Who?" I asked. "Who is it?"

He reached out with his long, thin finger and pointed. "You."

I stepped back, not even comprehending what he meant, my head spinning and my stomach sinking. "Me?"

He had compelled me to steal the aquoise stone, forcing me to betray the woman who had my heart. Now he wanted me to kill her?

I gritted my teeth. "I will not."

Draven's eyes darkened as he unleashed his purest self, lowering his glamour. His body stretched out until he towered over me with eyes darker than night, teeth sharper than daggers, and a hideous green-tinted face with an elongated nose and chin.

"**Hear me, Leaf,**" his voice bellowed, penetrating so deep inside of me I trembled all over. He had dropped his glamour in a rare display of power, and was now going to double compel me. My legs gave out under the weight of his command, and I fell to my knees.

"**You will gain the confidence of Princess Gabriela of House Strong. When I am ready to end the Strong legacy once and for all, I will show myself and issue this command which you must obey—End the line.**" He reached down and gripped my chin and lifted me off the ground. "**You will not remember a word of this conversation until you hear the command.**"

Draven's words echoed in my head, taking over my will, my thoughts, my desires. I saw nothing but him; heard nothing but him; felt nothing but him. He owned me in all things and controlled me completely. Nothing mattered but his words and his compulsion, and I lost all sense of time and space, not even knowing who I was anymore.

Darkness enveloped me. The pain from Draven's assault throbbed up and down my body, and my mind felt lost. Though I was alone in the dark dungeon, a strong feeling of unease wrapped around me like a vise.

Something was amiss.

I rose to my feet and scanned every nook and cranny for the source of my discontent, but found nothing. The last interaction I had with anyone was with Majestic, though that seemed a while ago.

Pressing my palms against the stone wall, I leaned over. Something had happened to me. Something dreadful, and Draven was the cause. I felt it in the pit of my stomach. Racking my brain, searching for any memory of what I had been doing after Majestic left me, I spotted a clump of green by my boot. I bent down and scooped it up, then studied it under the light. Trampled leaves. Lifting my foot, I examined the bottom of my boot and saw remnants of fresh dirt.

"Thunderation," I muttered, realizing I had been outside, most likely with Draven, and I had no memory of it. If he had taken that knowledge from me, then whatever we had done had to have been horrible.

Without a doubt, I knew it involved Gabriela.

16

GABRIELA

I kept my face pressed against Rook's back, my arms clamped around his waist, hanging on for dear life as the Enbarr held its top speed. Daring to peek every now and then, I only saw a blur of trees and brush. And when a splash of liquid sprayed my face, I peeked and saw water all around us, forcing me to hold on even tighter as I realized the Enbarr was racing across a lake.

After a while, and with every muscle in my body clenched tight, the Enbarr slowed down to a hard gallop that morphed into a trot before finally coming to a halt.

Uncle Manny slid off his ride first, moaning and groaning. "That sucked just as bad as the first time. Even in my new body. I can't even imagine what that would've been like as my old self," he said with a shudder.

Rook hopped off too, then helped me down. I walked around, stretching my arms and legs, my circulation slowly returning to normal. "I'll be okay if we never do that again."

"It is also my hope we will not need to do that

again," Rook agreed. "Enbarr are rare creatures and hard to find. We were blessed by the sun, moon, and stars that Adrius was able to summon them."

Adrius had dismounted and was stroking his ride, then said in a gentle voice, "Thank you, fine creature. We will go on foot from here."

The Enbarr stretched their long, graceful necks and shook their heads from side to side, nickering softly as they stepped away from us. Their pace quickened from a walk to a steady trot, then to an easy gallop through the trees, the rhythm of their hooves echoing softly before fading away.

Uncle Manny came up to me, and together we studied our new surroundings. Once again, we were enveloped by tall pines, concealed in the shadow of the branches and leaves. But this time, in the distance, the gold spires of Strong Haven Palace pierced through the canopy—glittering like promises and warnings all at once.

A chill worked its way down my spine. The palace was breathtaking, but knowing Draven roamed those walls made its beauty feel wicked. "That's really something," I murmured, awe and fear twisting together in my chest.

"It is," Uncle Manny said quietly. "I remember feeling so wowed the first time I saw all the gold and marble." He huffed out a short, nervous laugh. "Didn't think I'd ever find myself breaking in. Guess there's a first time for everything."

I managed a faint smile, wishing I shared his ability

to joke through fear. My stomach, however, refused to loosen its knots.

Rook stayed on task. "How do we get to the tunnel from here, Lady Sonia?"

She scanned the area. "There is an entrance not far from here. Once we are in the tunnel, we will wind through the underground passage for about two miles."

I reached back and adjusted my fighting stick, making sure it was snug against my back, while Uncle Manny adjusted his dagger. Verona and Adrius shifted their bows and quivers and fighting sticks too.

"If we are all ready, then let us make haste," Rook said.

Lady Sonia led the way. We followed her around several clusters of trees until we came to an area filled with berry bushes. She stopped near one and knelt down, running her hands around the dirt and lifting a latch that looked like a stick. A square chunk of dirt swung out, reminding me of a cellar door.

"It will be dark when we first enter, but as we move along, orbs will appear and provide enough light for us to see," she explained. "I know the way, so I will go first."

"I will go second," Rook said. "Then Lady Gabriela and Manny."

"Verona and I will take the rear," Adrius added.

Lady Sonia dropped down into the opening, followed by Rook, me, Uncle Manny, Verona, and then Adrius. When the opening closed, we were plunged into darkness. I reached out my hand and kept it on Rook's shirt while Uncle Manny kept his hand on mine.

We shuffled forward in a slow line, the air thick with the scent of damp earth and decaying leaves. Our shoulders scraped the walls, every step stirring loose bits of soil that brushed against our arms. After a while, the tunnel began to widen, and a faint glow flickered ahead—one of the orbs. We wound through the twisting path, light and darkness trading places as we passed from one orb to the next. With every step, my nerves climbed higher, a storm of doubts pressing in from all sides.

Would we be able to rescue Leaf and find the book before Draven discovered us? Was it even possible? After a few more turns, Lady Sonia slowed down and stopped in an area that was so wide we were able to gather together in a circle.

"Up ahead are two hatches," she said in a low voice. "Both lead to the cookhouse. One opens behind a shelf, and the other opens in the middle of the floor."

"We take our chances with the middle of the floor," Rook decided. "Emerging behind a shelf will be too cumbersome and loud."

"My thoughts too," Lady Sonia said. "Since Draven is now occupying the palace, it is likely he will have staff in there. I imagine they are serving him involuntarily. Therefore, they must remain unharmed."

"Yes, please don't hurt the staff," I agreed.

"But if they attack, they are dead," Verona said matter-of-factly.

"Only then," Rook admonished.

Uncle Manny moved in and asked in a hushed tone, "What do we do when we get in?"

"We split off into groups," Rook said. "Half of us will go for Leaf, the other half for the book."

"I'm going for Leaf," Verona and I said at the same time. We glared at each other, neither one of us changing our statements.

Rook interrupted our stare-off with a grunt. "Fine. You two are with me. The rest of you go for the book."

"I know the way to Lady Gabriela's bedchamber. If the book is there, I will find it," Lady Sonia said.

The orb floating overhead cast a glow on everyone's faces, revealing hardened expressions. As if we were about to go to battle. And for all we knew, we were. Draven was sure to have the palace heavily guarded.

"I will hop out of the tunnel first," Rook instructed. "Adrius after and then Verona. The rest of you, stay put until we give you the signal."

We followed Lady Sonia until she stopped a few paces ahead. She reached up, gripped a thick root jutting from the cave wall, and cranked it down like a lever. A low rumble shuddered through the tunnel as a circular section of earth and clay shifted overhead and swung open.

Rook moved first—vaulting through the opening in

one clean motion. Adrius and Verona followed close behind, their movements swift and silent.

The rest of us waited below, breath held, every heartbeat pounding in my ears. I strained to hear anything above us—shouting, metal, even a scuffle—but there was only silence. Too much silence.

Rook's shadow filled the opening. He leaned over, hand outstretched. I clasped it and climbed through, blinking hard against the sudden chill and open air. Lady Sonia and Uncle Manny followed right behind.

We emerged into the large open kitchen with wood shelves, a wooden table, and a large wood-burning oven. The smell of fresh-baked bread and spices erased the dirt-laden aroma from the tunnel. Three small maid servants dressed in white were standing with their backs pressed against the stone wall. Rook pressed a finger against his lips, motioned at the trio, then pointed at the opening.

They wanted to get out and must not have known about the tunnel.

Lady Sonia crouched down in front of them. "Take every right turn and you will find your way out."

Rook helped them through the opening, one at a time. The last one hugged his leg before scrambling out, then disappeared after the other two.

Rook brandished his dagger, as did Uncle Manny and Lady Sonia. Adrius and Verona readied their bows, while I unsheathed my stick and gripped it tight.

"Everyone knows what to do," Rook whispered. "Meet back here when the mission is completed. If you cannot return here, get as far from the palace as possible and head in the direction of the Sublands."

Cannot return? I gulped, and for the first time since everything happened, I thought we were doomed. Really and truly doomed.

Uncle Manny reached out for my hand and squeezed. "*Mija*," he said in a soft voice, channeling his older self and not his new younger self. "Please, be careful."

"I will, Uncle. You too."

We moved quietly out of the cookhouse, our footsteps barely whispering against the marble. Lady Sonia, Adrius, and Uncle Manny veered toward the stairwell, while Rook led Verona and me down a narrow corridor that twisted through unfamiliar parts of the palace. The air grew cooler, heavier, laced with the faint scent of damp stone and smoke. Every sound —the brush of fabric, the scrape of a boot—seemed amplified in the silence.

After several turns, we stopped before a thick wooden door. Rook gripped the handle, his brow furrowed. For a heartbeat, he hesitated. He looked back at us, eyes sharp with warning. "This is too easy," he whispered.

"I was thinking the same thing," Verona said.

My heart catapulted against my chest and I swallowed. "You think it's a trap?"

"Yes," Rook said.

"But we must continue," Verona said. "There is no other way."

"I'm with Verona," I said, thinking we had to get Leaf no matter what. "We have to keep going."

A long stretch of silence followed as Rook seemed to be considering all the options. "Agreed," he said. "We keep going. Everyone stay sharp."

We slipped through the door and closed it behind us, plunging into total darkness. Once again, I placed my hand on Rook's back, grateful for him to be with me and taking the lead, while Verona stayed close behind.

We took slow and careful steps, winding our way down a narrow staircase until we reached the ground. A thin stream of sunlight filtered in from an opening up high.

I was blinking, trying to adjust my eyes, when a voice spoke. "Who is there?"

My heart leapt. "Leaf, it's me."

"Gabriela?"

"And Verona," she said quickly. "We are here with Rook to rescue you."

"No, no, no," he pleaded. "You have to get out of here. It is not safe."

Ignoring his warning, we crept farther inside. The dim shaft of light from above cut through the shadows —and there he was.

My heart fractured. He was slumped in the center of the holding room, his skin streaked with dried blood, deep cuts crisscrossing his face and tearing through what was left of his clothes.

"Oh my gosh, Leaf," I whispered, the words breaking in my throat.

He clambered to his feet and shuffled away from us, his eyes filled with worry and even a touch of fear.

"Stop." He raised his hand. "Stay where you are. Draven has fashioned a magical barrier to keep me in. Save yourselves and leave this place."

His words flew right over me as I rushed in and slammed my hand on his wrist. "We are getting you out of here."

I pulled him with me, and his body crossed over with ease.

"Hurry," Rook rushed out.

He led the way and Leaf, Verona, and I dashed after him. We crossed the dungeon floor, flew up the steps, and found ourselves back in the bright corridor.

Leaf considered me with wide eyes. "What are you doing?" He leveled Rook and Verona with death glares. "What are you all doing?"

"You ungrateful fae," Verona spat. "We are rescuing you."

He dismissed her and pointed at Rook. "You know the code. If any one of us poses a risk to the others, then that person is lost."

"Stop," I pleaded, shocked that he had been tortured so completely he was not even himself.

He cast his eyes down. "I am lost. In every way." He stepped back, heading for the dungeon door. "You all should flee and leave me here. Please."

A clattering sound broke out, followed by the pounding of boots against the marble floor.

"Thunderation, Leaf. Enough of that. Get to the cookhouse," Rook ordered. "Now!"

Rook grabbed Leaf by the arm and yanked him forward, and we all started racing back the way we had come. The pounding grew louder while my heart hammered against my chest. We skidded to the end of the corridor and looked to the right as a barrage of arrows whizzed over our heads.

Verona spun around and unleashed her own volley of arrows in rapid fire succession.

"Keep going!" Rook shouted at me and Leaf, brandishing his dagger and staying close to Verona.

As if jolted to life, Leaf unsheathed Rook's fighting stick from his back, seized my hand, and pulled me into a run. We tore down the corridor, turning corner after corner until we burst into the cookhouse.

Lady Sonia was there, clutching the book to her chest, while Uncle Manny gripped his fighting stick and Adrius stood ready, arrow nocked and drawn.

"Stay here," Leaf ordered. "Adrius, with me!"

The two bolted out, disappearing into the chaos. My lungs burned, my pulse thundered. They were going to help Rook and Verona—but I could help too. I took a step forward, ready to follow, when a hand clamped around my arm.

"No, ma'am," Manny ordered. "You stay right here."

"But they might need me!"

"Manny is right," Lady Sonia said. "They would want us to stay out of harm's way."

I tugged my arm away from Manny's hold, but before I made another move, Rook, Leaf, Verona, and Adrius burst into the room.

"Go, go, go!" Rook yelled.

We sprinted for the tunnel opening. Lady Sonia leapt in first, I followed close behind, and Uncle Manny landed after me as the sounds of fighting thundered above.

"Keep going, *mija*! Don't stop!"

We stumbled into a wider area when Lady Sonia came to an abrupt stop. She dropped her bag at her feet and started rifling through her things. She drew out a small glass bottle, then faced the path we had just emerged from.

I sidled next to her. "Let me help!"

She lifted her brow, considering me for a few seconds, then nodded. "Place your hands on the wall. When our company runs past, I will throw this bottle. The explosion will be small, so I will need your power to help collapse the tunnel."

"My power?"

"Like your father. His blue energy. I have seen it," she said.

"Yes!" Manny encouraged me. "You can do it, Gabriela!"

With a hard swallow, I placed my hands on the cool dirt wall, not knowing if I could replicate a power like my dad's, but praying my Avila witchy skills would kick in.

"You got this," Manny whispered beside me. "Just concentrate."

Steadying my breath, I waited for Leaf and the others to charge through. "Collapse the tunnel," I muttered to myself. "Collapse the tunnel."

Verona burst into view, sprinting with everything she had. A heartbeat later, Rook, Adrius, and Leaf streaked past us in a blur.

Lady Sonia hurled the bottle, her voice cutting through the chaos. "Now!"

I squeezed my eyes shut and pictured the makeshift underpass collapsing—dirt and dust filling the air, the ground giving way beneath it.

Collapse, collapse, collapse...

A low hum built at my ears, swelling into a vibration that shuddered through my chest and gathered in my hands. The pressure mounted until it felt like my body would split apart. I opened my eyes just as a burst of blue light exploded from me, the force knocking me backward and stealing my breath.

Uncle Manny caught my arm and yanked hard. "Run, mija!"

We bolted forward as the corridor behind us gave way, the roar of collapsing stone chasing our heels. Dust and debris burst through the air, thick clouds of brown earth swallowing the passage in seconds.

"Faster!" Rook's voice cut through the chaos from up ahead.

We twisted and turned, sprinting for our lives, until we outran the falling passage and ended up in a part of the tunnel that was far enough away from the dust that we could see again.

"Stop!" Lady Sonia called out, coming to a halt. "There is an exit here."

She ran her hands over the walls, patting and prodding, while I leaned over and tried to catch my breath between bursts of coughing.

"Found it," she said. She pulled down a large root, and a square chunk of dirt opened above us. We crawled out and tumbled onto the grass.

Rook kicked the opening closed, then prodded us on. "We are still in danger! Keep moving!"

Leaf helped me up and we started running. With each stride, I kept thinking of those fantasy movies where the characters are forever running across valleys and even mountaintops. I didn't think I could keep up that kind of pace.

Uncle Manny echoed my thoughts. "How much farther?" he called out, huffing and puffing. "My new body isn't ready for this!"

Sparse trees were all around us, but ahead in the distance sprawled a thick wooded area. Rook pointed. "Over there."

We kept on, covering distance so fast, we were suddenly through the trees and in the shaded area. We started slowing when Lady Sonia moved to the lead. "Everyone follow me; there is a cave not far from here."

We continued on deeper into the woods until we

passed a thick brushy area that concealed an opening to a small cave. As soon as we filed in, Uncle Manny sank to the ground, breath ragged, while I turned to Leaf. I grabbed his hand and held it close.

"You're okay," I managed to get out between bursts.

He released my hold and stepped away from me, keeping his gaze down. "I am not okay."

"You are not," Lady Sonia agreed. "You are in great pain. May I take a look?"

He held his hands up. "Do not come close. Something is amiss with me."

Uncle Manny fumed. "Something is amiss with you? Really? That's all you gotta say after what you've done?"

Leaf tilted his head. "Manny?"

"Yes, it's me, Manny." He jammed his finger at Leaf. "And don't change the subject!"

"Enough of that, human," Verona hissed. "None of us can know what it is like to be in the clutches of someone as evil as Draven. We should all be grateful that we were able to rescue Leaf. So stand down, before I make you stand down."

"Hey, now!" I warned. "Don't talk to my uncle like that!"

"Everyone, stop!" Rook yelled. "Do you not think this was all too simple? Do you not wonder where Draven was while we were in the palace?"

"Oh," I muttered, shrinking back and thinking of the whole ordeal. "Well, maybe getting in was easy, but not getting out."

"Maybe it wasn't easy for someone from the human realm," Verona shot me with a look. "But for someone from this realm, our pursuers were weak."

"We handled them expeditiously, even though we were far outnumbered," Adrius chimed in. "With their numbers against ours, we should have been overtaken in the cookhouse."

Goose bumps raced across my skin. "You believe it was all... staged?" My mind reeled at the thought. "Is that what you're saying?"

"Perhaps," Adrius said.

"I am in agreement," Rook said.

"Wait a minute," Uncle Manny said. "You think Draven *wanted* us to rescue Leaf? *And* get the book?"

"The book, no," Lady Sonia answered. "No one was upstairs or anywhere near Lady Gabriela's bedchamber. But a group of guards who outnumbered us but did not stop us? There is meaning there."

I pressed my fingers to my lips, recalling the entire incident. "Leaf, you said Draven had a barrier holding you where you were, and that you couldn't cross over it. But I pulled you out of your cell with no problem."

Leaf took another step away from us, as if afraid to be near. "Draven must have dropped his barrier, then, because I assure you, it was there."

"Great," Manny muttered. "Just great. Now what?"

Rook pounded his fist against his open hand. "No matter how we are here, let us not forget that we are here! And Draven must be stopped!" He pointed at the book in Lady Sonia's hands. "We stick to the plan and locate the soul-stealing witches, the descendants of Keres the first soul vamp, and we figure out a way once and for all to end Draven the Witch. I want his head!"

I wanted Draven gone for good too, and the idea of the witches being able to help sparked hope inside of me, but then another idea sprang to mind. "Maybe they can help us figure out what's going on with Leaf too. Maybe we can learn something about his compulsion, and maybe even sever it. But we have to hurry. Draven could be coming here as we speak."

Rook held out his hand for the book. "Let us take a look."

Lady Sonia pulled the thick red leather-bound book close and her face hardened. "No one can examine this book. It is ancient and its writings are sacred."

"Huh?" Uncle Manny blinked. "I don't even know what that means. And who cares if it's ancient? We've got a situation here and we need answers that are in that book." He glanced at me. "Besides, Gabriela has already read part of it. So what's the big deal?"

Leaf had been standing away from everyone, but the discussion about the book piqued his interest. He raised his brow. "What claim do you have to the book?"

Lady Sonia swung around to face him, her long hair flowing behind her back. If I didn't know any better, I thought I saw something dark in her eyes. Something I had never seen before, like a shadow sweeping across her usually serene and peaceful demeanor. She held him in her stare for a few long seconds.

"My claim is that it is mine. I am Keres."

17

GABRIELA

Rook stepped back from Lady Sonia, his fingers curling around the hilt of his dagger. He drew it slowly, the metal whispering against the sheath, then leveled the blade between them. His dark eyes locked on the healer, cold and unblinking.

Beside him, Leaf shifted his stance, tightening his grip on the wooden fighting stick, muscles flexing at his neck. Adrius and Verona followed suit, steel flashing as they unsheathed their daggers. They hesitated only a heartbeat—eyes flicking between Rook and Lady Sonia—as if waiting for a silent order to strike.

Lady Sonia wasn't fazed by the show of force. She stayed calm and cool, her bag strapped to her back and the book in her hands.

"You are the soul vamp Keres?" I asked with a gulp, my mind reeling at the idea that after all these years, she was not who I thought she was. "The first soul vamp?"

"I prefer to be called a soul healer. But yes, I am Keres. But I assure you, I am not your enemy." She looked at each of us in turn. "You all would do well to lower your weapons."

"Someone who keeps secrets is usually an enemy, Lady Sonia," Rook said. "Especially a truth like yours that alters the fabric of one's being and one's alliances."

"There is nothing altered about who I am, I assure you. As for my truth, it does not belong to anyone but me and my sisters," she said coolly. "If I were indeed the enemy, you all would have been dead a long time ago. My alliance holds."

Uncle Manny threw his hands up in the air. "Whoa, whoa, whoa. Everyone just hold on a dang second. I've known Lady Sonia, or, uh, Keres, for a long time. She's the one who helped us subdue Draven and put him in the dungeon all those years ago. Rook and Leaf, y'all were there. You saw what she did. So when she says she's not the enemy, I believe her."

Lady Sonia had never been anything but kind and caring with me, and I regarded her as family. Every fiber of my being told me she would never hurt me. I moved closer to her, placing myself between her and Rook like a shield.

"I agree with Uncle Manny. I know who Lady Sonia is, and she is definitely not the enemy." I looked pointedly at Rook and then Leaf. "I think the two of you know we're right."

Rook eased his stance, slipping his dagger back in the holster at his waist. The others followed, standing down and lowering their weapons too. But from the look on Verona's face, she still wanted blood.

"Why, Lady Sonia?" Rook asked. "Why pretend to be someone you are not?"

She scoffed. "I am not pretending to be anyone. A name is nothing more than a label and does not change my identity. Who I am has always been the same."

"But your identity is that of a healer to the Strongs, not a deadly soul vamp named Keres," Leaf said.

"You know nothing of identity if that is what you think, Leaf of the Sublands," she admonished. "And nothing of the soul."

"You are not wrong there," he admitted. "I am a warrior, with no knowledge of spiritual matters."

She moved the book from one hand to the other. "Power can be used for many purposes depending on the intent of the user. There is light and dark, good and bad. Draven embodies all that is bad, sucking souls to bolster his own. He uses his gifts as a weapon, and the term soul vamp, or soul slayer, is rightly placed on him. I embrace the light and use my gifts for good. I am a healer in every sense of the word. A soul healer."

Even though her explanation made perfect sense, a million more questions filled my mind. Mainly, could her sisters help us fight Draven? And heal Leaf?

"What now?" I asked. "If the plan was to use the book to find Keres and her witch sisters so we could end Draven, then I can only assume the plan is off since we have found you, and now you won't show us the book."

"That is not what I am saying," Lady Sonia said.

I tilted my head. "Then what are you saying?"

She tapped the book with a finger. "My purpose for finding this book was not to hand it over to you, Gabriela. Or anyone else. This book belongs to me and my sisters. It has been lost for centuries and has vital information that must not fall into the wrong hands. As such, I plan to return it to its proper home. As for me and my witch sisters helping to destroy Draven, and possibly help Leaf, I am prepared to do just that, *with* the information herein."

I let out a sigh of relief, and I could hear Uncle Manny next to me doing the same.

"Oh, thank goodness. I was beginning to worry for a minute there." My shoulders began easing up some, but when I saw Rook, Leaf and the others still on alert, I tensed back up. "So what do we do now?"

"Now, you and Leaf will come with me to my home, away from danger and threats," she said.

"Unacceptable!" Rook shot out. "You will not be taking Lady Gabriela or Leaf anywhere."

"I'm with Rook," Manny interjected. "We need to stay together."

Sonia moved closer to me. "They must come. It is the only way we can determine if we can help end Draven and if we can heal Leaf's wounds and remove his compulsion."

Amid the cuts and the blood, hope sprang in Leaf's defeated eyes. He stepped forward. "You can remove Draven's compulsion?"

She nodded. "We can try."

My gaze met Leaf's. This time, he didn't turn away from me. His striking blue eyes held on to mine, and that was all I needed. "Fine, we'll go with you," I blurted.

Rook turned to me. "But Princess—"

"Don't do that, Rook," I pleaded. "If going with Lady Sonia will help us defeat Draven once and for all, and help free Leaf from Draven's clutches, then we're going."

No one said anything for a while, but I could tell my words had an impact. Rook backed down, and the hateful glare in Verona's eyes softened.

Uncle Manny broke the silence. "*Mija*," he said in a tender voice, "you don't have to do this."

"Of course I do. And I want to. For you, for me, for all of us." I gestured about the wooded area. "For all of Faevenly."

He came in and wrapped his skinny eighteen-year-old arms around me and held me for a while. "I love you, *mija*, and I'm so very proud of you. I know your mom and dad, wherever they are, are proud too."

Hot tears stung my eyes, and I clung to him harder, my chest shaking against his. For a moment, it didn't matter that everything around us had fallen apart—his arms still felt like home. "Thank you, Uncle Manny. I love you too."

We let go slowly, reluctant, like neither of us wanted to break the moment. I stepped back and took him in. His face was still jarring to look at—smooth tan skin unlined by time, dark eyes too bright for all they'd seen. Gone were the creases at his temples, the silver in his hair, the faint shadow of age I'd grown up with. He looked like a boy pretending to be my uncle, and no matter how many times I saw him like this, I couldn't quite get used to it.

Leaf still held Rook's fighting stick, and handed it back to him. I took mine off too and gave it to Uncle Manny. Then together we moved closer to Lady Sonia.

"Well," I said. "Now what?"

"Now, we go to my home," Lady Sonia said with slight nod.

"What of us?" Rook asked.

"You all will stay here. Time runs differently where we are going, so we will not be long." She studied the skies for a minute, then added, "Send a raven to Leto. Tell him to bring his strongest and most trusted warriors here as soon as possible."

"I will do it," Rook said.

She swung her backpack around and slipped the book inside. Her hand rose to the opal pendant at her throat, fingers trembling slightly as they traced the stone. With a sharp tug, light cracked open in the air and a hazy rim of shimmer appeared.

Her movements stayed fluid, almost ritualistic, as she drew the edges apart. The shimmer stretched wider, threads of light spiraling and bending beneath her touch. The air hummed, charged and alive, as the portal widened into a full circle that pulsed with soft radiance.

A gust of wind swept through, stirring her hair.

"Go," she urged me and Leaf, her voice calm but edged with strain. "Now."

With a small gulp, marveling that she'd kept such a vast shimmer hidden in something so small, I stepped forward. One last look at Uncle Manny—and then I crossed through.

A cool haze swept over me, wrapping my skin in a silken chill. It felt like the mist that rises off a lake after the wind has churned it, soft and alive, carrying the scent of rain and light. For a heartbeat, I was weightless —caught between two worlds—before my boots touched solid ground again.

My breath caught. Before me loomed the most breathtaking mountain I had ever seen. Its jagged, white-capped peak pierced so high into the sky that I had to tilt my head all the way back, and still, I couldn't see the top. Cascades of green swept down its slopes— rows upon rows of ancient trees—and nestled in their midst, a silver waterfall spilled in a narrow ribbon of light.

A crisp breeze rolled down from above, cool and clean, filling my lungs with air so pure it almost stung. The sky stretched wide and endless, not a single cloud to mar its brilliant blue. For the first time in days, I felt... small, and utterly alive.

"Incredible," whispered Leaf beside me.

"It is," I muttered.

Scanning the rest of the area, I noticed cottages tucked into the trees at the base of the mountain, and several women milling about. They wore long, flowing dresses of white, pink, and lavender. Some of them were carrying books, others baskets.

"This is my home," Lady Sonia said. "And where my family lives. We are safe here from any threat, so do not be concerned about Draven."

Leaf didn't make a sound or even move a muscle, but his nearness alone let me feel the weight lifting from him, his spirit easing. Still, I had to be sure.

"So we don't have to worry about Draven coming here and harming us?" I asked, almost afraid to hear the answer.

"We do not," she said.

"What about"—Leaf paused—"me harming anyone?"

A chill crept through me. *Him* harming anyone? I refused to believe it.

Lady Sonia shook her head. "You will not harm anyone here."

Her words were steady, but something in her tone —too careful, too controlled—made my stomach twist. I risked a glance at Leaf. Doubt flickered across his face, mingling with a kind of quiet vulnerability that undid me completely. Even bruised and broken, he was devastatingly beautiful.

She beckoned us forward. "Now please, follow me."

The crisp, cool air refreshed my heart and soul, as if nothing bad had happened to us and nothing bad ever could. In a surprise move, Leaf moved in close. He took my hand and laced his fingers between mine. Even though he was wounded and bloodied, his demeanor had changed completely. His heaviness disappeared and life and love sparked in his eyes.

"You're back," I smiled at him.

He squeezed my hand. "I am."

Lady Sonia led us to a one-story stone cottage. It had a wood-thatched roof with a tall skinny stone chimney. Smoke trailed out, reaching up to the mountaintop like a ribbon. A row of lavender bushes surrounded the perimeter, and windows with flowering plant boxes flanked the simple wooden door. Two small and slender ladies with long black hair, sharply pointed ears, lavender eyes, and long blue dresses walked over to us. One held a tray with fruits, cheeses, breads, and juice. The other held a tray with jars filled with different-colored liquids.

Lady Sonia pointed at the trays. "We are happy to provide you with food and drink, as well as healing liquids for the bath that will help with Leaf's wounds. Inside the cottage, you will find other things you might need, including a fresh change of clothes for both of you. Please take as much respite as needed. When you are finished, come find me."

Leaf and I gave Lady Sonia and the other ladies our thanks, then took the trays and entered the cottage. We found the inside as beautiful as the outside. Candles were lit on every surface, and a small fire crackled in a wood-burning fireplace in the corner of the room.

Shiny dark wood gleamed beneath my feet, its surface smooth and warm, while the walls shimmered faintly with the same pale stone as the cottage exterior

—almost as if the mountain itself had shaped them. A large bed draped in a thin white coverlet occupied one side of the room, beside a cozy sitting area with a blue sofa and a low table. Near it, a tub brimmed with steaming water, wisps of mist curling upward like whispers of magic. A row of windows lined the back wall, revealing the mountain's base bathed in soft light, timeless and breathtaking.

Leaf walked with slow and careful steps to the sofa, letting out a small grunt as he set his tray on the table. He needed healing relief from the liquids Lady Sonia had provided, and fast.

"Why don't you get those clothes off while I pour these liquids in the tub?"

He nodded, then carefully started peeling off his clothes while I opened the jars. One had thick green liquid in it, and I was pretty sure it was made from the healing waters. Purple water filled the other jar, and the soothing scent of lavender burst in the air when I opened it. I poured both jars in the tub. When every last drop was in, I turned to help Leaf and gasped. Cuts laced every inch of his body and purple bruises splotched across his skin.

I covered my mouth as my eyes watered over. "Leaf," I managed to say in a broken voice.

He shuffled over to me and placed his finger under my chin, lifting my head so he could kiss me. "It looks much worse than it is, my little princess. Though I am most looking forward to a healing bath."

He stepped into the warm waters, letting out soft

groans as he submerged all the way. When he came back up, he combed back his long dark hair with his hands, then eased back against the edge of the tub.

"Join me," he said.

After the incident in the tunnel with all the dirt, I wanted nothing more than to climb into the tub with him and clean up, and maybe even steal some kisses. But I was afraid to get too close because of his wounds.

"Are you sure it's a good idea?"

"I am sure."

I took off my shirt, my pants, and my underclothes, and slipped into the hot and soothing water. I waded across the tub to him, submerged like he had, then rose back up and settled myself beside him carefully.

His eyes were closed and his full lips parted ever so slightly. I studied his high cheekbones and the perfect curves of his face. Despite his wounds, he was still the most beautiful person I'd ever seen, and my heart ached for him in every way. I wanted to know what he had been through with Draven, longed to hold him to me and comfort him and soothe him. Wished for his wounds to heal and Draven's hold on him to disappear. Wanted nothing more than to feel his body against mine and be with him completely. But more than anything, I wanted us to be rid of Draven.

Forever.

Sitting near him, a sinking feeling wormed its way through me and settled in my gut that all the things I wanted were impossible.

18

LEAF

Draven's darkness swirled deep inside me. It filled my head and clouded everything I knew about myself, stripping me down to such a vulnerable state, I could not think. Could not even form an independent thought. Could barely even see the world as it once was.

When Gabriela, Rook, and Verona stepped into my dungeon, I did not want to go with them. Draven controlled my every thought, and fear ruled me so completely I wanted to stay. But Gabriela, the girl who had my heart, yanked me forward, doing for me what I could not do for myself.

She saved me.

Now, we were in Lady Sonia's homeland, a place so magical I almost felt like myself. As if the very air had wiped Draven from me. Deep down inside, though, I could still feel the lingering traces of the mad witch's darkness.

Could Lady Sonia really rid me of him? Could she truly abolish his compulsion? Learning she was Keres, the first soul vamp, or as she preferred to be called, soul healer, gave me hope.

Soaking in the therapeutic water with my little princess at my side, I rested while my body healed. The liquid stung at first, irritating my shredded skin. But after a while, a relieving numbness took over, like a calming drug. Giving myself over to the sensation, I allowed my body to do what it wanted.

Rest.

TIME DID NOT EXIST WHERE I HAD DRIFTED. INDEED, nothing existed. No wounds, no war, no evil, no Draven. Only peace and serenity. Though I longed to remain in that blissful state, I could not. I needed my princess.

I slowly opened my eyes, one after the other, but did not see Gabriela in the bath with me. Peeking over the edge of the tub, I spotted her sleeping on the bed and wondered how long I had been soaking. I plunged myself under the water one last time, then got out and grabbed a towel from a nearby table. Drying myself off, I realized my cuts had healed completely. I ran my fingers over my arms, then my chest, and found my skin perfectly smooth. I brought my hands up for a closer inspection, searching for scarring. But not a mark could be seen.

Feeling healed and rejuvenated, I snuffed out the candles, but left the small fire burning in the fireplace. Wanting nothing more than my little princess, I climbed into bed and snuggled up beside her, burying my face in her soft hair that smelled like a summer garden. She moaned and turned to face me, her eyes fluttering a bit before they opened wide.

"Leaf," she breathed.

"Gabriela," I answered, sweeping a strand of hair away from her face and tucking it behind her ear.

She sat up, and I did too. Her eyes roamed my face, my neck, and my chest. She reached out and placed her hand on my cheek. "You're completely healed."

"I am," I said, feeling stronger than ever, though I could still feel Draven's nagging darkness lurking somewhere inside of me. Somewhere buried deep. But Gabriela did not need to know that. We had a lot to discuss, but now was not the time.

Tracing the side of her face with my fingertips, I studied her beautiful sun-kissed skin, her full lips, and her seductive mahogany colored eyes that filled with tears.

"Please do not cry for me," I whispered.

A tear slid down her face. "I thought you were broken. I thought I had lost you." She trembled as another tear slid out.

I wiped her tears away, thinking she was the sun, the moon, the stars, and the sky itself, and I did not want to ever be without her. "I am not lost. Not in this place. I do not know how or why, and I do not know what will come of me when I leave here. But right now, I am me."

She hugged me with fierce intensity and I wrapped my arms around her, never wanting to let her go. We stayed like that for a while, so still and silent, immersed in each other's closeness and warmth, until she slowly pulled away.

"I have so many questions," she said, wiping her cheeks. "So many things I want to know about what happened to you."

"If I can, I will answer them." I held her petite hands, threading my fingers through hers, marveling at the beauty of her sunshine skin next to my moonlight, waiting for her to ask me what she wanted to know.

"Can you tell me anything about what Draven did to you?" Her voice came out low, her tone giving away her fear.

I focused my thoughts and searched my mind for answers, remembering only a few things. "I know I was held, I know I had a visitor named Majestic, I know assassins were sent for you, and I know I was attacked." I shook my head from side to side, unable to recall more. "I do not know anything else, and even those things are fragmented. Like distant memories."

"I guess that's just as well," she muttered.

I raised her hand to my mouth and kissed her palm. "What about you and the others? How did Manny transform? And how did you come upon Adrius and Verona?"

Something crossed her face, like a shadow. I did not mention it, but instead waited for her answer.

"Well, we fled Strong Haven and headed for the Sublands, but they turned us away. We ended up going to the manor in the west, but then those assassins came. We fought them off and fled into the woods. That's where Verona and Adrius met up with us and where Lady Sonia made a healing potion for Manny that accidentally reversed his aging."

I kissed her palm again. "That is quite the tale. I am glad you all made your way safely to me."

She shifted her body, and I detected a slight change in her. Something was on her mind. I waited for her to tell me.

"Leaf, can you tell me about Verona?" She drew her hand away from mine and started picking at the bedsheet. "She seems really intense about a lot of things, including you."

There it was. The thing that was bothering her. I scooped her hand back up in mine and held it tight. "I have known Verona for most of my life, and I consider her as a sister, though there was a time when she wanted more."

"She wanted a relationship?"

"She did, but I did not. My rejection caused her great pain. And although we have found a way to coexist, she still harbors feelings for me."

"Oh," she muttered. "That must be hard for her."

"It is her choice, and there is nothing I can do for it." I traced her arm with my fingertips, not wanting to think of anyone else—needing only her, here, now. "What I want and desire in every way is you, Gabriela. No one could ever compare. You must know that."

Her gaze softened, luminous and sure. She cupped

my face in her hands, her touch light as starlight. "Then show me."

"If that is your wish, my princess, my queen," I whispered, "I will gladly obey."

I drew her close and kissed her slowly, savoring the warmth of her lips, the sweetness of her breath, the quiet rhythm of her heart against mine.

The world around us faded until there was only her laughter caught between our kisses, her hands tracing paths of fire along my skin, my arms around her as if holding something too precious to ever lose. Time blurred, and our hearts found their own language.

In that stillness, nothing else mattered. She gave me all of her, and I gave her all of me—not just my body, but my soul. And if I could give her my life, I would.

A GENTLE WARMTH WASHED OVER MY FACE, DRAWING ME out of my deep and restful sleep, beckoning me to arise. Opening my eyes, I saw soft daylight pouring in from the windows. I turned to my side expecting to see Gabriela, but she was not there. Nor was she in the room. Scanning my surroundings, I spotted a change of clothes for me at the foot of the bed and a fresh bath.

Flinging off my covers, I plunged myself in the warm pink-colored water, but did not stay in long. I needed to find Gabriela and then, of course, Lady Sonia. There was much to discuss.

Dressed in the dark pants and green shirt that had been provided, and slipping on my boots that had been washed and polished, I exited the cottage. Not too far off, I spotted Gabriela and Lady Sonia sitting on log benches around a small fire. When I joined them, Gabriela scooted over with a smile and patted the bench for me to sit next to her.

"Good morning, ladies," I said with a nod.

Gabriela slipped her arm around mine and smiled. "Good morning."

"Good morning, indeed," Lady Sonia said. "I see your wounds are healed."

"They are. Thank you, my lady," I bowed my head. "I am most grateful."

"Look at the waterfall in the mountain," Gabriela said, pointing ahead.

The waterfall stretched from the top of the mountain, and must have emptied somewhere in the mountain cavity, because I did not see it end. Admiring its beauty, I realized the water was not rushing down, but appeared still, like a painting.

I raised a brow. "It is frozen?"

"It appears frozen, but it is actually flowing at a high rate of speed," Lady Sonia explained. "Time passes differently here. The speed of the water is not visible unless one is very close."

"Incredible," I muttered.

"I know, right?" Gabriela said. "I didn't even notice until Lady Sonia pointed it out."

I took my attention away from the waterfall and eyed the tall, thin, dark-haired healer. "Lady Sonia," I began, "is that what you would like us to call you? Not Keres?"

"I have gone by many names over time, but yes, Lady Sonia is the name I am using right now."

Gabriela glanced at me, then inched forward. "So... you're the first soul vamp? I mean, soul healer," she said. "The one I read about in the book?"

"I am the first, yes," Lady Sonia said softly. "I am Keres—the one you read about in the book."

For a moment, the air seemed to shift. Lady Sonia's calm composure carried an old sorrow, the kind that clings to every word. Her eyes glimmered with the weight of centuries lived and lost, of memories she'd long since buried.

"I know you mentioned the difference between a soul vamp and a soul healer," Gabriela said, breaking the hush. "But can you explain more about that? How did you end up the way you are—and how did Draven end up the way he is?"

"Of course. The simplest explanation is that a healer mends, a vamp takes, and I have never taken," she explained. "Now, let me explain that further, as it will help you understand who I am as well as who Draven is."

"Draven," Gabriela uttered. "Know your enemy."

"Yes, Gabriela. Like your father and Uncle Leto

have taught you. Know your enemy." She folded her hands on her lap and drew in a deep breath. "When the world was young, and I was but a girl, I lived with my family in a small village of witch healers. We were a peaceful people, communing in harmony with nature, and kept to ourselves.

"One day, war broke out across the land. My people tried to stay out of it, but war is hard to avoid. Unfortunately, it found us one evening while we were asleep. We did not have time to take up arms, nor to use our magic. Many of us perished, and I was badly injured, holding on to life by the thinnest margin."

Gabriela wore a confused expression and cleared her throat. "But Lady Sonia, that's not what the book said. According to the book, you and your sisters were raised by harpies in a dark and wicked forest."

"The book you found and read contains tales that have been passed down for generations. Some of the stories are accurate, others embellished, and some of the facts are out of order."

"Out of order?" I asked, leaning forward. "How so?"

"You will see," she said, continuing on. "As the book correctly explains, my sisters, desperate to save me, gave me the blood of a unicorn. As the most magical creature in all of Faevenly, it is believed unicorn blood has the purest and most potent healing properties. My sisters took only a bit, with permission of course, and fed it to me. When I finished the drink, what we thought was a unicorn shifted into a demon, its real form. That is when we discovered the true nature of what I had consumed."

She paused, giving us time to absorb her tale. "The realization of what we had done broke me and my sisters. We were devastated and ashamed, but none as much as I. Worse than that, with our village destroyed, my sisters and I had no place to go. As luck would have it, a harpy came upon us and offered us refuge in her forest. Her name was Madga. She was lovely and wise, unlike most harpies, who are ugly and cruel. She is the one who told me I could take people's souls, because she had seen the trickster—the demonic shapeshifter —do it."

"What about Draven, then?" I asked, imagining the cruel witch wanting to drink a demon's blood. "Did he come upon a demonic shapeshifter too?"

"He did not. He came across me. I am the one who turned him."

Gabriela covered her mouth and gasped. "No."

The healer nodded in silent answer to Gabriela's denial. "My sisters and I were traveling one day when we came upon a carriage that had overturned. The occupants had perished, save for a young boy. He was barely holding on to life, and looked so frail. I was not sure if I should save him. Part of me said not to interfere, but I could not ignore his desperate pleas. Neither could my sisters. Knowing the healing properties of my blood, I gave him some so that he would live. I did not think he would turn out differently than me. I thought we would be the same, but something in him perverted it and made him who he is today."

"You created him," I uttered, envisioning Draven's wrongdoings, remembering his sinister presence in the dungeon. "You are responsible for all of this."

She closed her eyes, as if lost in what she had done, then opened them. "I am. Not a day goes by that I have not agonized over that fateful decision. There was no way for any of us to know what Draven would become."

I released Gabriela's arm and rose to my feet, pacing in a circle and struggling to keep my anger in check. "When you found out, why did you not try to end him? Why did you let him continue his reign of terror?"

She drew in a deep breath, as if steadying herself. "His transformation moved slowly. A hateful glance here, a wicked move there. I did not think evil would permeate his entire being. When my sisters and I finally discovered the truth of what he had become, he was grown and had been away from our forest and our influence for many years. Later, in an effort to right my wrong, I tried to stop him but discovered that because my blood revived him, I could not end him. My hand would not strike, and my powers were rendered useless when it came to him."

A small gust of wind swept over us, picking up the flames. The tongues of fire lengthened with a crackle and a pop, then died back down when the wind stilled. Gabriela reached out to me and pulled me next to her.

She held my arm, keeping me close, and turned to face Lady Sonia. "I understand the guilt, and I understand the remorse. And I'm grateful that you've told us everything, but what do we do now? How do we defeat Draven?"

"There is the question," Lady Sonia said. "My sisters and I have been thinking long and hard for a way to end him, and the only thing we have come up with is for another soul vamp to take his soul. Someone who can get close to him."

"Like who?" Gabriela asked.

"Like me," I said, avoiding a glance Gabriela's way and stopping Lady Sonia before she could offer up any other suggestions. I longed to end the devious witch, and this was my chance. "I will gladly do whatever necessary to kill Draven, though you will need to change me first."

"What?" Gabriela asked, stunned. "You can't be serious, Leaf. Not after everything he's done to you!"

"A quarrel is not necessary," Lady Sonia added quickly. "And I am most grateful for your offer, Leaf. My initial idea was indeed to remove your compulsion, turn you, and have you perform the deed. But after consulting with my sisters, we agreed that if your compulsion is removed, Draven will know, and he will end you in an instant. That leaves only one other person who can get close enough to the deadly witch."

I squeezed Gabriela's arm and moved her close to me, knowing exactly where the healer was going with her words. "Do not even say it," I hissed.

"I am sorry, Leaf. Truly I am. But the only person who can do it is Gabriela. She is the answer."

"No," I growled. "I do not accept that! Gabriela is not stepping foot near that monster, do you understand? Not one foot!"

I was so enraged, I did not sense Gabriela releasing my hand, did not notice her standing up, until she spoke.

"I will do it."

Lady Sonia rose to her feet and placed her hands on Gabriela's shoulders. "Thank you, Gabriela. I would not have suggested it if I did not think you were equipped to perform the task. Especially now that we know you carry the same magical power as your father, as evidenced in the tunnel." She released my shoulders and stepped away from me. "I will leave you and Leaf to discuss things. Come back to this fire when you are ready to proceed, and I will join you."

When Lady Sonia left us, I walked away from Gabriela, unable to bear the sight of her after she'd volunteered for something so dangerous. The weight of her choice pressed against my chest like armor I could not remove.

She approached quietly, her steps soft, hesitant. "Leaf," she murmured.

"I do not think you know how much I love you," I said, my voice breaking in the middle.

She cupped my face in her hands, her touch gentle but trembling. "Please, don't do that. I *do* know how much you love me because I love you the same. That's why I'm doing this. Ending Draven once and for all is the only way we can be together, and the only way Faevenly can ever be free." Her gaze locked on mine, fierce and unwavering. "But if I'm to succeed, I'll need your help and your faith."

I pulled her into my arms and held her close, my heart pounding against hers. Her warmth, her scent, the steadiness of her breath—each one branded itself into my memory, because I knew this might be the last time I would feel them.

I buried my face in her hair, whispering the only truth that mattered. "Then I will help you, even if it ends us."

And as I held her there in the fading light, I knew it already had.

19

GABRIELA

My mom and dad had always taught me to be tough and brave, but after that conversation with Lady Sonia, I felt anything but. And I hated it. Still, if this was my fate, then I'd face it head-on. If volunteering to be turned into a soul vamp meant a death sentence, then fine. I'd rather go down in a blaze of glory than in a heap of tears.

I pulled away from Leaf's desperate embrace, every part of me aching to stay there a little longer. But I couldn't. Not when the world was falling apart. "If I'm going to beat Draven, I can't be vulnerable or emotional. I need to be a confident and strong warrior. Like you."

He blinked. "Like me?"

"Yes, you. You're the most skilled fighter in all of Faevenly, right? So that means you're fearless. I need to be fearless right now, more than anything." I held his hands in a firm grip. "Will you help me?"

He breathed deep, studying me for a while before finally giving in to my request. "Yes." His face hardened. "I can help you with fearlessness."

"Good." I kissed him on the lips, feeling scared as

hell but also hopeful. "So how do I do it? What's your secret?"

He crossed his arms and thought for a while. "For me, I suppose the key to being fearless is two-fold—knowing I'm better than everyone else, because I am, and not caring what happens to me."

I tilted my head. "Not caring?"

"Yes, not caring if I live or die makes me fearless. At least, that is how I used to think. It has been admittedly harder to not care now that you are in my life."

His words hit something deep inside me, catching me off guard. He cared that much? For me? My chest tightened, warmth and fear tangling together. Could I ever be that selfless—care so much for someone that I'd stop fearing death altogether? I doubted it.

But I had to try.

"You already have the knowing-you-are-better-than-anyone-else part accomplished," he pointed out. "You have incredible powers and the ability to sense impending danger. You can even talk to spirits. No one in Faevenly is like you."

"My dad is..." I said, my voice trailing off. "He's like me. Or, I'm like him. But he's in the Passing Place with my mother." Lady Sonia had told me not to tell anyone my dad was alive, and so far, I hadn't. But I wanted to tell Leaf, needed to confide in someone.

"I am so sorry about your father, Gabriela."

My thoughts filled with memories of my mom and dad as I lowered myself back down onto the log. Leaf joined me, and I scooted closer to him. "You don't have to be sorry about my dad, because he's actually alive in the Passing Place with my mother."

His brows stitched together. "He is what?"

"He is alive. He can't leave because my mother doesn't know she's dead yet. But now I'm thinking I need to get him."

"Of course you do, Gabriela," he rushed out. "I have seen his gifts."

My gaze drifted to the burning fire. "The last time I tried to connect my mind to my parents and went to the Passing Place, they weren't there."

"They were not?"

"No, they weren't. I looked for them, and I couldn't find them."

His gaze took on a faraway look. "What do you think that means?"

I shook my head. "I don't know. But now that I'm here in this magical place, I should probably try to see them again. Maybe I can find them this time."

He stood and helped me up. "I think that is a good idea. Let us go to our lodgings for privacy."

Back in the quaint and cozy cottage, we found the bed freshly made with lavender-colored linens, the fire still burning, and a tray of breads and cheeses with fruit on the table. I ignored the food, feeling way too tense to eat, and went over to the bed.

"Is the magic you use to connect with minds the same magic you use to go to the Passing Place?" Leaf asked.

"Yes, it's the same."

"How do you use your magic? How does it work?"

I sat on the edge of the bed. "I'm not an expert and I'm still learning, but I usually concentrate on where I want my mind to go and then it happens." I scooted back on the bed, then lay back.

"What should I do?" Leaf asked.

"Nothing. Just stay here with me."

He leaned over and kissed my lips. "I will be right here."

He backed away from me, yet stayed on alert with sharp eyes and a ready stance. I drew in a deep breath, then closed my eyes. The last time I had tried to connect with my dad, I had focused on the lavender fields and bright sky of the Passing Place. This time, I decided to turn my thoughts to my dad.

Just him, and nothing else.

Julio Avila, thick dark hair, salt and pepper along the temples, tall, muscular, and fit. Completely and totally in love with Mom, caring and protective. I envisioned him teaching me how to fight, jogging around the lake with me, and helping Mom with her recipes. I could practically see our kitchen and smell the herbs.

Tumbling in my thoughts, a weightlessness came over me, followed by a plunge. When it stopped, I opened my eyes and found myself in some place entirely different than I had intended... my Austin home.

The house teemed with family members, which made sense, because whenever one of us was in a crisis, or needed something, the Avilas gathered and cooked.

My *abuela* was in the kitchen, stirring a big stainless steel pot of what I assumed was *caldo*. Several of my aunts and uncles were near, chopping cilantro and onion, while my cousins sat around the kitchen table playing Mexican Train, our favorite family game. One of them was Aliana.

I glided through the kitchen and made my way over to the stove, marveling at how none of them had noticed me, when my *abuela* looked in my direction and screamed.

"*¡Mija!* Gabriela!"

She dropped her spoon and rushed over, stopping in front of me, tears streaming down her face. Her hands passed through me as she tried to hug me. "*¡Dios mío!*" She made the sign of the cross from her head to her chest and then shoulder to shoulder, and so did everyone else in the room. "Where are you? What is happening? Where are your parents and Uncle Manny? I have been worried sick!"

"Oh, *Abuela*. Things have been awful. I'm so sorry I haven't tried to communicate with you sooner." I shuddered at the thought of telling her everything because I knew it would destroy her. So I decided to stick to the bare minimum. "I'm still in Faevenly with Uncle Manny. But my mom and dad," I swallowed, "are in the Passing Place."

"Passing Place?" Her brows stitched together. "*¿Qué es eso?*"

The lump in my throat grew thick, the words to explain everything floating in my head. What should I say? I edged closer to her, wishing I could hold her. "It's the place where people go when they die."

She brought her hands to her mouth with a gasp. Her entire body shaking. "They have both died?"

Whimpering and gasps broke out in the room as the family gathered around *Abuela*, catching her as her knees buckled and she sank to the floor.

I fell to the floor in front of her, my hands hovering over her body and trying to grab her too. "*Abuela*, no! My dad is still alive!" Tears gushed from my eyes. "It's my mom," my words caught in my throat. "She's gone."

Abuela reached a trembling hand to my face as her own tears flowed down her dark and wrinkled face. "*Mija. Mi pobrecita, mija.*"

If my heart hadn't shattered before, it did now. Seeing *Abuela*'s reaction, I felt the loss of my mom deep in my core all over again. As if I hadn't really felt it before. And I knew I would never be the same.

My uncle Trent held my *abuela* tight and looked right at me with shock and grief. "Are you sure, Gabriela? Are you sure your mom is gone?"

I tried to wipe my face, my hand passing right through. "Yes," I said in a half whisper. "I'm sure."

Uncle Trent's head hung low for a few seconds before he slowly brought his stare back to me. "What is happening in Faevenly?"

Abuela sat up straight, using the dish towel draped

over her shoulder to dry her eyes. "Tell us," she said. "Tell us everything."

"I'm about to confront Draven the Witch. He's responsible for everything. I wanted to see my parents before I did because I need my dad's strength, but my mind brought me here instead."

Abuela leaned forward. "You have his strength. It is already in you. *Siempre*. Since the day you were born. All you need is faith."

"Faith," I repeated.

She tilted her head, her eyes warm and steady. "Yes, faith is a warrior. Remember?"

My chest ached, and I pressed a hand over my heart as if to keep her words inside me. "I remember."

"Good," she huffed, her strength and resolve returning. "Now, go kill that witch, and then get yourself and your dad home."

I smiled. "I will, *Abuela*."

"Finish it, Gabriela," Uncle Trent said in an angry voice. "We will all be here sending you our love, and our prayers, and our power. There is great strength in our family, and in you."

"Thank you, Uncle Trent. Thank you, *Abuela*. I love you both so much." I scanned the faces of my family, some of them clearly able to see me while others couldn't. "I love you all."

I stood and stepped away from them, my mind focusing on Leaf and our cottage. My hazy body slipped away from my family home, and I opened my eyes to find myself on the bed with Leaf leaning over me.

"Gabriela," he said in a worried tone. "Are you all right?"

I sat up, my body trembling, my face wet with tears. I clutched the cross at my neck, thinking of my family in Austin praying for me. "I'm okay."

"What happened?" he asked. "Did you find your mother and father?"

"No, I didn't. I ended up in my home and saw my *abuela*. She's safe with my aunts, uncles, and cousins. They reminded me that I'm strong and told me to have faith. The last thing my uncle said was to finish it."

"Finish Draven?" he asked.

"Yes." I met his gaze, the words tasting like resolve on my tongue.

"Well then," Leaf said, his voice low but certain, a flicker of pride glinting in his eyes. "I think you should do what he says."

"I think so too," I said, my mind processing what it meant to finish Draven. "I guess we should meet with Lady Sonia now so she can turn me." My stomach plunged thinking about the procedure, recalling all the vampire movies I'd seen over the years. "How does that even happen?"

"I do not know, but if Lady Sonia was turned by drinking the blood of the demon shapeshifter, and Draven was turned by drinking Lady Sonia's blood, then I am assuming you will need to drink blood too."

I shuddered. "I was hoping you wouldn't say that, but I think you're right."

Leaf grabbed my hand and helped me to my feet. "Let's go find Lady Sonia."

We left the cottage and went back outside. But before heading to the fire, I held Leaf back.

My gaze scanned the coven paradise. "I want to take all this in for a minute, if that's okay. Everything here is so beautiful and peaceful and serene, and who knows if we'll ever come back." I wanted to say who knows if we'll survive this, but I desperately held on to my newfound courage and the idea that I could actually beat Draven.

"Since time runs differently here, we do not have to rush. Let us take a walk," he suggested. "It will do us well."

We strolled down a path that led us to a large round water well, and around that the most magnificent garden of all kinds of fruits and vegetables. Deeper in the forest, quaint and cozy cottages resembling ours were staggered among the trees.

We continued on, getting closer to the mountain, its majesty looming over us like a godly monument. The lush green grass thinned out the closer we got to the base and was replaced by brush and trees. Picking our way through, we found a boulder with a flat top a stone's throw away from the waterfall and climbed on top. We sat down and settled in, as if watching our very own movie. My gaze swept up and down the water, examining it for movement but not seeing any.

"Do you see it moving?" I asked Leaf.

His blue eyes examined the flow. "I see small sparks that I believe are movements. Let me show you."

He raised my arm and stretched out my finger, pointing at what he was seeing. Following the line and searching the blue and white stream, I saw a fleck of light.

"I see it," I said with wonder. Holding my gaze, I saw it again. "Amazing."

He lowered my arm, but kept his hand laced with mine and we didn't say anything for a while.

"What if we stayed here?" he asked, playing with my fingers. "And be together forever in this place?"

A small laugh escaped my lips. "I would love that, more than anything, but you know we can't."

"I know," he murmured. "It was only a dream I had."

A long sigh escaped my lips. "A wonderful dream."

He had finished playing with my fingers and had moved on to running his hand up and down my arm. But this time, a wave of sorrow crossed his face. "You must remember, Gabriela, that when we return, Draven's influence on me will be restored."

I hadn't wanted to think about that, but he was right, and I hated it. I shifted closer to him and straddled him, wrapping my legs around his waist and threading my fingers through his long, soft hair.

"Before we leave this place, I want to look at you, Leaf. Really and truly study every inch of you before we become something we don't recognize."

He sat still as I touched his forehead, his eyelids, his nose, his cheeks, his mouth. His hands copied each movement as he caressed my face in turn, his eyes brimming with tenderness and emotion.

"I do not even know how I have fallen so fast and so completely for you, Gabriela Avila, daughter of Strong Haven, but I have." He brushed his lips against mine. "It is as if I was fashioned for you, and you were fashioned for me."

"Soul mates," I said. "In the human realm, we call that soul mates."

"Mated souls," he said, placing his hand over my heart. "Yes. I feel that I am mated with you physically and spiritually, for all eternity."

"I feel it too."

We kissed again. This time, we didn't stop, couldn't stop. We stripped off our clothes in a flurry of passion and longing, exploring each other's bodies entirely and intimately under the canopy of nature and creation. We touched everywhere. We kissed everything. We opened up every last bit for the other. And when we had nothing else to give, we held on to each other.

20

LEAF

W e stayed together for a long while, neither of us wanting to break away from the other, until eventually we had to.

"I guess we should go now," Gabriela finally said, rising to her feet.

I stood too, but had no words because I did not want to go, could not bear the thought of the danger she was putting herself in. But I knew her mind was set.

Dressed and ready to face what was next, Gabriela and I locked hands and made our way in silence back through the village and to the fire where we had met Lady Sonia earlier. We lowered ourselves on the logs. Still we did not speak. And we did not have to. We had shared everything and had pledged our love to one another. Our existence even. Now, all that was left for us to do was end Draven.

But Gabriela would have to transform into a soul vamp first.

We sat close, watching the flames crackle and pop, when Lady Sonia joined us. She wore a solemn look on her face and held a small vial filled with red liquid.

A small gulp came from Gabriela. "Is that... your blood?"

She nodded. "It is. I have also added a few herbs and spices to help it go down smoothly."

"Thank you, Sonia." She released my hand and reached for the vial, but stopped midway. "Wait a minute. If you couldn't stop Draven because you and he shared the same blood, and I'm about to drink your blood, won't that mean I can't stop him either?"

"My sisters and I enchanted the mixture so that it does not form the same kind of link. So you should be fine."

I gently lowered Gabriela's arm. "The word *should* offers no assurances, Lady Sonia."

"That is true in this regard, but also true in life. Assurances do not exist. Ever. That is why I do not offer them."

Gabriela turned to me and held me in her gaze for a few long seconds. "She's right, Leaf. There are no assurances in life. But I have to do this right now. I know that for sure." With a slow exhale, she faced Lady Sonia and took the vial. "I have faith in you, Lady Sonia. And your sisters."

"And we have faith in you," she said in a solemn tone.

Gabriela lifted the vial to her lips and drank it in one gulp. When she finished, she handed it back to Lady Sonia. "That wasn't as bad as I thought it would be. But what now? Am I going to feel any differently or get sick or anything?"

"No, you will not get sick. In fact, it will be the opposite. You will start feeling more robust," Lady Sonia answered. "As if performing at your optimal level."

I considered Lady Sonia. "What do you mean, robust?"

"One benefit of being a soul healer, or soul vamp, is feeling strong and powerful. Invincible, even."

Gabriela raised her eyebrows. "Really?"

"Yes," Lady Sonia answered. "It will serve you well as you go up against Draven."

"That's good to know," Gabriela said, "and an added bonus. I guess all that's left for us to talk about is how to actually take a soul."

"It is quite simple," Lady Sonia explained. "You must get close to Draven's face so that your lips will almost touch." Lady Sonia brought her palms together, but stopped them within a hair of each other. "When you are in position, you will suck his air out of him. If his lips are closed, you will need to pry them open."

"Pry his lips open?" Gabriela shuddered so hard her entire body shook. "That sounds not so simple. And awful."

"It is not a difficult task," Lady Sonia assured her. "Once you are close enough, your instincts will kick in and you will know exactly what to do."

Gabriela exhaled, blowing out a long stream of air. "Get close to his mouth and let my soul vamp self take over. Got it."

The day had started to darken. And while Gabriela

and Lady Sonia continued discussing the nuances of being a soul vamp and what Gabriela would need to do when we returned to the others, my mind drifted to what would become of me when we left this place.

Draven had compelled me—that I knew for a fact. His order was clear. Find and take the aquoise. With that accomplished, I had no idea what he had in store for me next. Though I did know he had something in store. His touch lingered in the back of my mind.

Lady Sonia had said she could not remove the compulsion because Draven would know and end me summarily. But I was beginning to think I should not go back with Gabriela. That my presence would be a risk to the mission. That Draven would use me to do something terrible and make me tell him everything I knew, and I would have no choice but to obey.

"Leaf," Lady Sonia said in a calm and soothing tone, pulling me from my thoughts. "What would you like to say?"

My mind must have been so loud it alerted her to my plight. Perhaps she could help me. "I do not want to jeopardize Gabriela in any way, or the others. I cannot help but think, with Draven's hold on me, I will be a liability." I inched forward, a new idea forming. "Is there any way for you to erase from my mind what has happened here?"

She shook her head. "There is no need. The compulsion ceased working on you when you stepped through to my homeland. This place has its own sort of protection. Anything that transpired here cannot be taken from you."

Gabriela squeezed my hand. "Thank goodness."

I squeezed back, but had one more question for the healer. "Is there any way for you to ascertain what Draven has in store for me?"

She shook her head sadly. "There is no way." She folded her hands on her lap, keeping her attention fixed on me. "But I can say that I have thought about your role in all this and your connection with Draven. I sense his darkness in you. But through the darkness, I see your light. It is there and you must not forget it."

I let her words linger in the air before I asked the question that was burning inside of me. "Will I jeopardize Gabriela?"

Gabriela tightened her grip on my hand as Lady Sonia's eyes closed ever so briefly. "It is not yet written. You must let the future unfold and see it through."

"Hey," Gabriela said, nudging my knee. "I'm willing to take my chances on you. I'm willing to take the risk."

I pulled her in and kissed her forehead, already knowing I would not let her bear the risk. "Thank you, my princess."

Lady Sonia rose to her feet. "It is time to return to the others. Are you both ready?"

"We are," we said at the same time.

She touched the stone on her necklace, pulled out her shimmer, and stretched it long and wide. Gabriela passed through first, and then Lady Sonia. I scanned the magical mountain before stepping through, hoping that maybe Gabriela and I would come out of this intact and come visit here sometime.

Maybe.

21

GABRIELA

W hen I stepped through the shimmer, I found my Uncle Manny standing in front of the cave opening holding an armful of branches and sticks. His eyes flew open and his mouth dropped. Everything tumbled out of his hands as he rushed over to me.

"¡*Mija!* What happened? Did the shimmer not work?" He patted my shoulders and then my arms, as if expecting to find a wound or something. "Are you all right?"

I took his hands and squeezed, grateful to have him with me. "I'm fine, and it totally worked. We've been gone two full days. Now we're back."

He blinked. "Really? When Lady Sonia said time ran differently over there and that y'all would be back quick, I didn't think it would be *that* quick."

"How long has it been over here?" I asked, searching for the others.

"Not even five minutes. Rook issued his usual orders and we all started gathering wood, and then bam, here you are."

Lady Sonia came through the shimmer behind me,

followed by Leaf. Uncle Manny did a hard double take at the tall, dark-haired fae. "Leaf?" He walked over to him, looking him up and down in disbelief. "You were trashed and cut up and bleeding. Now, you're as good as new?"

The troubled look in Leaf's eyes had returned, letting me know that returning here brought back his struggles with whatever Draven had done to him. Just as we had feared.

"Yes," he answered in a stiff voice. "Lady Sonia and her people healed my wounds."

Rook, Verona, and Adrius came into the clearing carrying their own stacks of wood. When they spotted us, they set their stuff on the ground and came over with questioning stares.

"That was indeed quick," Rook said. "How did you fare?"

"We fared well," Lady Sonia answered. "There is much to discuss."

"Excellent," Rook said. "I see that Leaf fared especially well." He nodded in Leaf's direction. "I am relieved to see you are healed."

"Thank you, Rook."

Rook scanned the thick trees and the darkening skies. "We will build a small fire, then discuss what happened in Lady Sonia's homeland so we can figure out our next move. Time is of the essence."

Scooping up the twigs and branches with Uncle Manny, I thought of how tired I was of fires and woods and sleeping on the ground. Even if this time we had a cave to sleep in. But then I told myself it wouldn't be long before all of this was behind us. Would I miss it? But then a worse notion came to me... would I even be alive? Would the others? I had already lost my mom.

Trying to erase my morbid thoughts, I kept my stare down and my hands busy, but my thoughts went back to who in the group wouldn't make it. Suddenly I caught myself locking eyes with Verona. I quickly looked away, feeling terrible that I wouldn't mind her dying.

"What is wrong with me?" I muttered to myself.

"Nothing, *mija*," Uncle Manny muttered back. "Nothing at all."

I flashed him a smile. I always could count on Uncle Manny to support me, even when he didn't know he was supporting me.

We worked in silence, stacking the wood and tucking in twigs and brush. With everything in place, Rook got busy rubbing a long stick between his thick hands, starting at the top and working his way down to the base. After a few tries, a flame sparked, and soon we were sitting around a small fire.

"I suppose I should begin the conversation," Lady Sonia said. "But first, I must ask Leaf to consume something that prevents him from hearing us."

"That is fine with me," Leaf said.

Lady Sonia began rummaging through her bag. She brought out something that looked like a small piece of bark and handed it to Leaf. He took it swiftly, popped it in his mouth, and swallowed it. Then he wandered away from the group, my heart breaking at seeing him so changed.

"Gather close," Sonia said.

Like the lights dimming before a play, a hush fell on the rest of us as we huddled around the fire and gave Lady Sonia our attention.

"As everyone can see from Leaf's appearance, the wounds he sustained from Draven have been healed. But what you cannot see is that whatever hold Draven has on him remains."

"What? But why?" Verona shot out angrily. "I thought you and your people could help him." Rook silenced her with a glare and she sat back with her arms crossed.

Lady Sonia explained. "Lady Verona, as I was about to say, if we had meddled with Draven's compulsion, Draven would have known and more likely than not, would have ended Leaf with his magic. We could not take that risk. The other thing you should know is that my sisters and I agreed that the best way to end a soul vamp is by using another soul vamp."

"Like head to head?" Uncle Manny asked. "Is that even possible? And can we even find one?"

"Yes to all of that," Lady Sonia said. "We need our soul vamp to get close enough to Draven so that they can take his soul from him and end him once and for all."

Verona clenched her fists on her lap. "I will gladly do my part to help this soul vamp get close to Draven."

"I will as well," Adrius said.

Rook nodded with satisfaction. "We all will. Now, who is this soul vamp and when will they be joining us?"

Silence settled over the fire. Lady Sonia drew in a breath but didn't speak, her gaze sliding toward me.

My stomach dropped. I cleared my throat. "The soul vamp is already here. It's me."

I had seen Uncle Manny's eyes bulge before, but never like this. If he could have lost his eyeballs, he would have. He jumped to his feet. "Are y'all serious?" He pointed at me and Lady Sonia. "Have y'all lost your ever-loving minds?"

"Uncle Manny, it's not like that. Being a soul vamp is not a bad thing. I mean, yes, a soul vamp is bad, but there's also a good side of it called a soul healer. In this one thing, with Draven, I will be a soul vamp. But then after, I'll be a soul healer, and a soul healer is good."

He buried his face in his hands for a minute. "*Mija*, I'm your *padrino*. I made a promise to your parents and to God at your baptism to take care of you if anything ever happened to them. And now you're not even you anymore!"

"Uncle Manny," I said, feeling scared that he was right, "don't say that."

"I assure you, Lady Gabriela is still herself," Lady Sonia added in her calm and soothing voice. "Only now, as a soul healer, she has the ability to help count-less others. It is a gift to be a soul healer."

I looked up at my uncle and saw the war in his eyes — the part of him that wanted to fight this, and the part that only wanted me safe.

"Fine," Uncle Manny muttered, lowering himself back down, as if giving in and figuring out there was nothing else he could do or say. "I don't have to like it, but I will always stand by you, *mija*. No matter what."

I placed my arm around him and gave him a hug. "I know."

"You honor us, my lady," Rook said. "I thank you."

With a nod to Rook, I said. "I'll do anything for us, and for Faevenly."

Lady Sonia continued with the final part. "Now we must figure out a way to get Gabriela close to Draven so she can end him before he ends us and her."

"Without getting her killed," Uncle Manny chimed in. "Let's not forget that."

"Her, or any of us," Rook added.

"We cannot use the tunnel system, because we have destroyed it," Adrius said. "Right, Lady Sonia? Or is there another way in?"

Lady Sonia was on her feet, pacing in a small circle. "I do not know of any other secret way in."

"Nor do I," said Rook.

While the team strategized, my attention drifted to Leaf over by the entrance to the cave. He was sitting on a log now, clenching his hands together on his lap and keeping his gaze on his boots. Worry lines raced across his forehead. I wanted nothing more than to go to him and comfort him, but now was not the time.

As if sensing me watching him, he lifted his stare and met my gaze. Turmoil and despair penetrated his eyes as he slowly shook his head from side to side. I had no idea what that meant, other than it wasn't good. He rose to his feet, and I rose to mine, as if my standing would prevent him from saying whatever he had on his mind.

"With my hearing returned, it is clear to me that I must go now," he announced. "Draven is in my head and I cannot escape him. If I stay, it will only jeopardize things."

As if everyone around us faded away, I stepped closer to him and he to me. "Please don't do this."

"Gabriela," he pleaded. "I have no other choice."

I shot Lady Sonia a desperate glance. "There must be something we can do to help him."

"There is nothing," he said, answering for her. "I am dangerous. You know that, and so do the others."

Uncle Manny piped in. "I know. Let's tie him up. That way he can't harm us, and Draven can't harm him."

Rook stitched his brows together. "Will that work, Lady Sonia? Binding him?"

"Draven has great power, but I believe it might work."

"Then do it," I blurted. "Right now. There's no way in hell we're letting him go, only to be taken again by Draven."

Lady Sonia sifted through her things. She brought out a thin silver string. "This is a binding cord I keep with me at all times. Anyone wearing this will not be able to move their hands and will thus be rendered harmless."

A surge of hope rushed through me. "Will it really work?"

"It should," Lady Sonia said.

Leaf marched over and held out his hands. "Do it. Bind me."

She looped it around one of his wrists, crossed it over, then looped it around the other, muttering some sort of spell under her breath. Then she tied the ends of the string together. When she released her hands, the string flashed bright white, faded back to silver, then transformed into one seamless piece.

Leaf inspected Lady Sonia's handiwork. He yanked and jerked his hands, trying with all his strength to pull the string apart, but couldn't. Satisfied with his binding, he stepped back with a bow of his head. "Thank you, Lady Sonia."

Instead of joining us around the fire, he returned to where he'd been sitting and resumed the same posture. Head down, hands together. Everyone went back to where they'd been sitting too, but not me. I moved closer to Leaf and sat next to him.

"Everything is going to work out," I said, leaning my head against him.

The flames of the fire had started to wane, shrinking to a low glow. Adrius eased himself from his spot and tossed in a handful of sticks and leaves. The flames shot up, brightening the area, revealing a fluttering thing high above. Like a tiny bird. Which was weird, because birds don't fly around at night. At least not the ones in the human realm.

"Everyone, look," I said, pointing.

The bird neared. As it got closer, I was able to see that it wasn't a bird after all but a tiny sprite. The one that had come to us with Leaf's message when we were at the Strong Haven Manor.

Leaf rose to his feet. "Majestic?"

"Lovely Leaf, I have found you! And you are healed!" she exclaimed in a small, high-pitched voice. He held out his hand, and she landed on his palm with a step. She frowned at the cord around his wrists and brought her tiny branch-like fingers to her mouth. "Oh my, oh my! You are once again a prisoner, by your own friends? I am so frightened!"

"No, no. It is not like that. I have allowed my friends to bind me so that I will not hurt them."

She lowered her hands. "I do not understand, but if you say it is all right, then it is."

"It is. Thank you, beautiful sprite. How did you ever find me?"

We had all gathered around, mesmerized by our tiny visitor, listening to what she had to say.

She smiled, looking pleased with herself. "I tracked your lovely scent. It exudes the sweetest smell of lavender, cedarwood, and geranium. I followed it from the palace, across the meadow, and here to these woods. It was imperative I find you."

"You are most talented, Majestic," Leaf said.

She smiled again, but not for long, because her tiny face took on a sad and worried expression. "I have come to tell you of the utmost atrocities that are happening at the Strong Haven Palace."

Leaf's brow furrowed as he scanned our faces, then turned his attention back on the gold-winged sprite. "What is that mad witch doing now?" he seethed.

"Oh, Lovely Leaf, and Lovely Leaf's friends, Draven the Witch has destroyed the shimmers of Torch Lake. I saw him, and I was so frightened! Before I flew away, I heard him say he had another plan, something sinister to do with the waterways that will hurt all humans! But I could not hear what. I am so very sorry."

Leaf's eyes darkened and his face hardened as anger oozed from him.

Rook matched Leaf's fury with his own. "Thunderation," he spat, turning around and slamming his fist against a tree trunk. "We must kill that mad witch! We must be done with him!"

Uncle Manny's tan face had turned almost white. "Humans," he muttered. "That's us, Gabriela."

"Many in Faevenly have human blood," Leaf said. "Me included, remember?"

Fear plastered Majestic's tiny face. "I am glad I found you, Leaf, so that you all may save yourselves. But now I must go. I am so very frightened and must return to my woods."

"Thank you, Majestic," Leaf said. "You are a brave and honorable wood sprite. I hope to see you again someday."

A yellow-hued tinge touched her brown tree-bark cheeks as she fluttered toward Leaf and kissed his forehead. "I hope so too." Then she twirled and flew up and away.

"Well," Uncle Manny said, looking terrified. "If we weren't scared as hell before, we should be now."

He was right. I was absolutely scared as hell, but I was also formulating a plan. Verona and Adrius were too, because they started talking about marching over at first light to scope out the palace. Uncle Manny chimed in, arms crossed, demanding we try to form an alliance with another province. Even Lady Sonia joined the heated discussion.

"Stop!" Rook shouted. His deep gravelly voice silenced the group like a slap. "I have sent word to Leto, and he sent word back. He is on his way and will be here in the morning. He claims to have found a way to end Draven once and for all and wants us to strike tomorrow evening under the cover of darkness. I was not to mention anything until his arrival."

Lady Sonia's brows lifted, but she kept her silence.

Uncle Manny smiled and nudged me with his arm. "There you go. Leto will find a way to handle this whole thing."

I studied everyone's somewhat surprised and relieved expressions, but found a different look altogether on Leaf's face. He appeared confused, even lost. I took his hand.

"What is it?" I asked.

He waited a few seconds before he responded. "It is nothing."

I didn't believe that for a minute, but didn't want to question him. I squeezed his hand. "Hold on, Leaf. All we need to do is make it through the night and then Leto will be here. Everything will be better then."

22

LEAF

The second I stepped out of Lady Sonia's homeland and back into the woods, the inkling of Draven's dark influence returned. Like an unwanted visitor, I felt him ever so near, as if he were watching me, listening to me, influencing me. Even with the magical bindings on my wrists, I knew I would be a liability to the group. But the tipping point for me was knowing Leto would be arriving with a plan.

Draven's evil knew no bounds, and it would only be a matter of time before he used me in some sort of dark way. If I knew Leto's plan, Draven would force it out of me. Which only meant one thing—I needed to leave Gabriela and the others and get as far away as possible.

Our small fire cast a faint glow in the dark woods as everyone retired for the night in the cave. I chose a spot away from the others, closer to the outside. Nobody seemed to mind, except for Gabriela. I knew she wanted to be close to me, but I would not let her. As for the others, deep down they understood my reluctance to be near.

The night crawled by as I waited for the perfect

moment to steal away. I focused on everyone's breathing, waiting for the long pause between inhale and exhale. When the moment was right, I raised myself to a sitting position. I stayed that way for a few moments before rising to my feet. Standing perfectly still, I waited a few seconds more before I took my first step, then another, making sure to pace myself and step as lightly as possible. With the distance between me and the others increasing, I picked up my speed.

Emerging from the tall trees, I spotted the looming gold spires of the palace in the distance. They sparkled against the backdrop of the night sky, like magnificent beacons, issuing me a warning to get away. Which was exactly what I planned.

I turned, following a straight path away from the palace, hoping that if I traveled far enough, Draven would not be able to reach me. With each step, anger and loathing for Draven swirled inside me as I envisioned Gabriela defeating him once and for all.

But my steps did not carry me far enough at all as a voice saturated my mind.

"**Halt!**" Draven roared.

My legs stopped. My breathing stilled. A rush of panic and fear flooded my senses while I waited for another command.

"**Come to me,**" Draven ordered.

A tug pulled at me, forcing me to turn around, my body operating on a command that was not my own. Draven had me in his clutches again, and I was headed straight for him. With the bright moonlight lighting my course, I marched forward until I neared the manicured grounds that surrounded the palace. I was almost upon the sprawling stone patio when I saw a figure shrouded in darkness.

Tall. Lean. Dressed in all black with the lightest skin and devious sparkling white eyes. I came to a halt before Draven the Witch.

I let out a breath I had been holding and growled, "Draven."

He stepped out of the shadows, his black cloak drifting behind him. "Leaf, I am glad to see you looking so well and so refreshed." He reached out with his long finger and trailed it along the side of my face. "It is a marvel you look so... you." He glanced down at my wrists. "Tsk, tsk, tsk. Your friends do not trust you?"

I kept my silence as I shot daggers with my eyes, refusing to answer him.

"No matter," he said. "They may not trust you, but I do." With a wave of his hand, the binding fell to the floor. He kicked the cord away with his boot, then edged in close to me. He drew in a long, deep inhale. "Ah... delicious. I smell the little princess."

I exploded with rage, struggling to strike out, but unable to. He slammed his hand around my throat.

"**Stop**," he hissed, his voice traveling through every molecule of my being, taking away my will. My body went slack, my muscles weak. "You are mine, and your feeble attempts to break my hold are futile. Understood?"

"Understood," I said, my voice acting on its own.

He released his hold with a smirk, then dusted off his hands. "Follow me to the Great Hall. I would like to treat you with honor as you tell me everything your friends are planning."

He led me into the palace, along the corridors, and into the Great Hall. The floating orbs along the ceiling cast a low glow, shrouding the place in a sinister light. He motioned toward a long wooden table. I moved forward and sat on one of the chairs. He sat across from me, resting his arms on the smooth wood, and laced his fingers together.

"**Tell me everything**," he commanded.

No matter what I wanted, the words spilled out of me. "They sleep in a cave not far from here—Gabriela, her uncle, Lady Sonia, Rook, Adrius, and Verona. Leto has sent word that he will rendezvous with them in the morning. He has a plan to strike at nightfall."

"Hm, is that so?" He tapped his fingers on the table. "Nightfall?"

"Yes."

"And you, cloaked in your honor and nobility, thought you could leave so as not to betray your friends?" He leaned forward. "Is that right?"

"That is right."

A wicked smile lengthened across his face. "How awful for you to be such a betrayer." He backed up his chair and rose to his feet. "I must prepare for their arrival. In the meantime, you will stay here."

He left the room with a swish of his robe, and all I could do was wait.

23

GABRIELA

A shake at my shoulder woke me, pulling me from a hard and deep sleep. Peeling my eyes open, I saw Rook hovering over me.

"You must arise. We have a new course."

"A new what?" I asked, sitting up and looking around. A fresh fire was burning and the others were stirring. Wondering what time it was, I peered out the cave opening, but only saw moonlit darkness.

"It's the middle of the night," I muttered.

With a rub of my eyes, I scanned the area where Leaf was, but he wasn't in his spot. I climbed to my feet and searched all around, but he was nowhere to be seen. My heart started picking up speed as alarm spread through me.

"Where's Leaf?" I asked out loud to no one in particular.

Uncle Manny was still on the ground but had started rolling over to get up. "Huh?"

"Leaf," I said with a hint of panic in my voice. "Where is he?"

"Gone," Rook answered.

"Not long ago," Lady Sonia continued.

My stomach dropped. "Gone?"

Verona spun around while Adrius moved from one side of our camp to the other, searching for signs of Leaf.

"He has left in an attempt to not betray us, as I knew he would," Rook said. "There is no use looking."

Bewildered, I approached him with careful steps, still not believing what he had said. "You knew?"

"Of course I knew. I have known Leaf since he was but a small child. I know him better than he even knows himself. He would not want to jeopardize you or our mission, so he did what he thought was the most honorable thing. He left. Thus, in his mind, protecting our cause. And you."

Verona fumed. "But we are still foiled, then. Draven no doubt has Leaf by now, and Leaf knows Leto is coming and that we will be heading to the palace after the next sunset. He will tell Draven and we will be doomed before we even arrive."

Rook crossed his arms. "We will not be doomed because we will not be arriving after the next sunset. We are going now."

Lady Sonia picked up her bag and slipped it on her back. "I could tell you were up to something, Rook. Good work."

Up to something? I shook my head, not even under-standing what was happening. "Wait a minute, we are going now? What about Leto?"

Rook shifted his weapons in place, his fighting stick

on his back, his dagger at his belt. "I sent word to Leto but have not heard back."

I furrowed my brows, still so confused, remembering all the things I'd been taught about the fae. "But fae can't lie, Rook."

With his stuff in place, he turned to face me. "I am not fae. I am human."

My mouth fell open and I gasped, taking a few steps back. I didn't even say anything for a minute as my mind processed his words. "You're what?"

"That's right," Uncle Manny muttered. "I actually forgot about that."

I stepped closer to Rook, examining his long dark hair and looking for signs of pointed ears like all the other fae had, but his hair was too thick. Then I studied his smooth face.

"I-I-I don't know what to say. I mean... You look like a fae, on the muscular side, but still a fae. And if you were here when my parents were, how have you not aged?"

Rook gave a quick explanation. "Lady Sonia made a tonic for me that allows me to age at the rate of a fae. As for my ears..." He pulled his long hair back. They were pointed, but scarred. "Lord Cailean of the Sublands found me when I was a boy and shaved them so I could blend in."

I gulped. "I-I-I had no idea."

"Of course you would have no idea. Only humans indulge in idle talk. Who I am needs no mention."

Verona and Adrius started loading up their fighting

sticks and daggers, then slung their bows and quivers behind their back. It was obvious they knew about Rook, because they didn't even react.

"We are ready," they said together.

I had left my fighting stick with Uncle Manny when Leaf and I had gone with Lady Sonia, and he handed it back to me.

"Here, *mija*."

"Thanks," I muttered. I slung it on my back, shifting it around until it fit perfectly, still feeling so stunned that Rook, who was actually human, knew Leaf would leave and had fed Leaf false information to give Draven.

It was an impressive move, but didn't change the fact that Leaf was with the witch again. My stomach clenched at the idea of what Draven was doing to him.

Pulling me away from my thoughts, Rook went back to issuing orders. "When Leaf is taken, he will tell Draven our plan. Draven will believe him because Leaf is under Draven's compulsion and cannot lie even if he wants to. They will not be expecting a move from us tonight."

"We will have the element of surprise," Verona said.

"Exactly," Rook said. He crouched down, picked up a stick near the fire, and started drawing a rectangular shape with a large front door and a row of spires on top. He drew an identical shape but with three smaller doors. He pointed with his stick at the first drawing. "This is the front of Strong Haven." He pointed at the second. "This is the back." He handed me the stick. "Where is the largest bedchamber?"

"The second floor has all the bedchambers," I said. "And the biggest one, where Leto and Pen lived, and before them the High King and High Queen, is at this corner overlooking the largest fountain in the garden." I marked the spot with an *X*.

"That is where Draven will be," Rook said.

"So how do we get in?" Uncle Manny asked.

Verona pointed to the corner of the palace. "Someone can easily climb in from here."

I pointed to the bedchamber where I used to stay, the bedchamber that belonged to my mom when she was young. "I used to climb from my bedchamber down to the garden late at night all the time when I was little. There's a lattice under the window, so it's super easy."

Adrius pointed at the back. "Verona and I will pick off any guards from the rear."

Rook eyed me. "And Gabriela and I will climb in."

"Uh," Uncle Manny said. "What about Lady Sonia and me?"

"We will monitor the entrance and take care of any guards in the front of the palace," she said with a confident nod.

Rook folded his muscular arms. "Does anyone have any questions?"

Uncle Manny rubbed his hands on his pants. "Nope." He glanced at me for approval and I gave him a shrug. "No questions from us."

With that settled, everyone returned to their tasks of gathering up our things. Uncle Manny moved in close to me.

"How are you feeling about all this?" he asked.

On the one hand, I was ready to finish what had been started and do whatever I could to end Draven's reign of terror once and for all. But on the other hand, I feared we would be the ones ended.

"I'm feeling okay, I guess," I answered, deciding to keep all my doubts to myself.

Uncle Manny rubbed my arm, signaling he understood the turmoil within me. "I know. I feel the same."

Rook kicked the dirt around, erasing our drawings, then tossed a chunk of dirt on the fire. He grunted as he stared off in the direction of Strong Haven Palace.

"May the sun, the moon, and the stars guide us to victory."

I placed my hand on my shirt where my cross hung and said to myself silently, "Amen."

24

JULIO

Every day was the same as the one before. Celyse and I napped in our favorite meadow, ate the fruit we picked, and went fishing.

But today felt different.

I was lying on my back on the soft green grass, watching a slow-moving puffy white cloud drift across the bright blue sky. Celyse was sitting next to me, running her hands across the blades of grass. She plucked a daffodil from the nearby wildflowers and stuck it in her hair over her ear. Then she plucked another one and stuck it over mine.

"You are lovely," she laughed.

"As are you," I said with a smile.

Reaching out with my hand, I rubbed her back, my attention still on the cloud as it continued its slow journey. The idea of it moving on somehow struck a chord of melancholy within me, and I had no idea why.

Celyse plucked another daffodil. She brought it up close and studied the yellow petals. "I feel like I should give this flower to someone."

I turned to my side to study her and saw sorrow in her magical green eyes. "Who do you think that is?"

She carefully stroked the small petals and shrugged, looking lost in her thoughts. "Someone beautiful and special."

"You already gave me one," I said with a smile.

She pushed my shoulder. "Yes, you are beautiful and special, but I was referring to someone else."

The sound of a whinny followed by the soft clomping of horse hooves interrupted us. I sat up next to her and watched as a gorgeous white steed pulled a trailer across the meadow, heading toward the horizon.

"What is that again?" she asked.

I rubbed my chin. We had seen another horse and trailer like that a few days ago. Or was it months ago? I wasn't sure. "I don't really know."

We stayed sitting like that, mesmerized by the rhythmic trot of the horse and the steady rolling of the trailer wheels as it traveled farther away, looking smaller and smaller until it blended into that spot where the sky meets the earth.

"Hmm," I said. "I wonder what was in that trailer."

Celyse didn't answer. It was as if she was entranced by the horse and its cargo, mesmerized by its very passage. I rested my head on her shoulder and asked, "Did you hear me?"

She turned to me and kissed my cheek. "What were you saying?"

"I was wondering what was in that trailer."

"I wonder too," a small voice said.

We shifted around and saw a small boy with blond

hair approaching us. He had sharply pointed ears, silver eyes, and wore an all-white outfit.

"My goodness," Celyse said with wide eyes. "Who are you?"

"My name is Filly." He fidgeted with his collar. "Who are you?"

"I am Celyse and this is Julio."

"Hello, Celyse and Julio."

"Hello, Filly," we said.

He scratched his head, looking around for a few seconds, then asked, "May I sit here with you?"

I patted the grass and shifted over some. "Of course. Please, sit."

He plunked down in front of us and crisscrossed his legs. He didn't say anything for a while, and neither did we. We were too surprised by his presence.

"How long have the two of you been here?" he asked.

"We have been here..." Celyse's voice drifted away. She rubbed her forehead, then turned to look at me. "How long have we been here?"

My mind searched for the answer, sifting through my thoughts, but I couldn't come up with it. So I settled on a simple response. "Not long."

The young boy studied the daffodil in my hair, then the one in Celyse's. He plucked a flower of his own and threaded it over his ear. The corners of his mouth turned up with glee. "How does it look?"

Celyse smiled at him. "It looks splendid."

He continued picking the flowers and gathering them up in his hand. "I think my mother would like these."

"Your mother?" Celyse asked.

"Yes, my mother."

I considered him with a puzzled look, because we were the only ones in the field. In fact, I hadn't seen another person around. "Where is she, Filly? Your mother?" I asked.

He shrugged as his smile faded. "I do not know. I have been looking for her and my father."

Sadness swept over Celyse's face, and she reached out and touched the boy's shoulder. "I am so sorry, Filly. But I do not think there is anyone here but us."

He kept picking flowers, growing his bouquet, not seeming too worried at all. "That is not so. I saw a girl here not too long ago. She was looking for her mother and father too."

I sat back, surprised to hear the boy had seen someone since Celyse and I hadn't seen anyone. Celyse and I flashed each other questioning looks.

The boy stopped picking flowers, happy with his arrangement, then rose to his feet. "I have to keep looking for my mother and father now. I hope to see you two again."

He turned to walk in the same direction of the horse and trailer, but something inside of me said to stop him and ask him about the girl he had met. As if it was important, and we needed to know.

"Filly," I called out, rising to my feet. Celyse stood with me.

The boy turned around. "Yes?"

"The girl that you saw here. Do you happen to know her name?"

"Oh, yes. Her name was Gabriela. She was pretty and nice, and we talked and then she left."

He continued on with his flowers in his hands, his words working through me like that cloud I had seen. Slowly drifting across the fabric of my mind.

Gabriela... Gabriela... Gabriela...

The name repeated in my head over and over and over until I suddenly remembered everything. Gabriela was our daughter. And Draven had attacked us.

I crashed to my knees, the truth of everything collapsing on me in a horrifying rush. Celyse fell to her knees too, the terror-filled look in her eyes telling me she also remembered everything.

"I am dead," she muttered between breaking sobs. "Draven killed me."

Knowing the truth changed everything. In a blink, I was solid and she was translucent, and I couldn't touch her anymore.

"Oh, Julio," she sobbed.

With tears streaming down my face, I wrapped my arms around her, my arms passing through her hazy form as I cried with her. We stayed like that for a long time, our forms close but unable to make contact as heartache and utter devastation rooted us in place.

We cried for what we had lost. Cried for all the things that would never be. Our tears could have filled a thousand oceans.

Neither of us wanted to move, or leave the other, but eventually we knew we had to. She pulled back and said again, this time as if accepting it, "I am dead. And you are alive."

I wiped my face and nodded, unable to speak.

My sun and moon and stars had been taken from me. I leaned in and stayed as close to her as possible, yearning for her touch and not wanting to leave her space. She was everything to me.

Her hands hovered over mine as she tried to hold them and I tried to hold hers. "Celyse," I managed to whisper as a flood of heartache clogged my throat. "My love."

She moved in again, as if resting her forehead against mine. After a few long seconds that could have lasted an eternity, she pulled back and opened her magical green eyes, newfound resolve shining through as the princess in her emerged.

"My beautiful husband. You have to go back. You need to find Gabriela. She needs you."

"I know," I managed to say. "I know."

She rose to her feet, and I did too. She glanced in the direction of the creek. "You did not want me to venture past the creek and to the lake. Do you know why?"

Somehow, in my state of suspension, I wouldn't let myself remember what I had done in the lake, because knowing and telling meant I had to leave her. But with my new awareness and with the fog lifted, I remembered. And it was finally time to let her know.

"I know why," I whispered.

"Will you tell me?"

"I will show you."

We took our usual path through the hedge and to the creek, picking our way over fallen branches and piles of leaves. I started explaining as we walked. "When Draven attacked us at the palace, we were standing at opposite ends of the corridor. He flung an energy blast at you, and you disappeared."

"I remember," she muttered.

We reached the bank of the creek and followed it to where it widened into the lake. I motioned her forward. "Our forces charged in, and when they distracted Draven, I used your shimmer to find you."

I tapped my gold wedding ring, where I kept the shimmers Lady Sonia had made for me—one for Celyse, and the other for Gabriela. Celyse had her shimmers in her ring.

We walked a few more paces, and I stopped when we reached the sandy lake entry. "Your shimmer brought me here. At first, when I saw you, I was so relieved because I thought you were okay. I thought we'd made it."

I brought my hands up to her hazy face. "But when I looked closer, I noticed the translucent sheen. The wavering edges. The slight glow." Tears clogged my throat, but I swallowed them down. "I knew you were a spirit. I had seen so many, I had no doubt. But you... you didn't know. I couldn't tell you because if I told you, you'd leave me. And I couldn't bear that. I wasn't ready. And so I stayed, and over time, I forgot you were no longer alive."

"Oh, Julio," she whispered, her eyes welling up with glistening tears.

We stayed together like that, caught up in our emotions, but there was one more thing to share. And she knew it.

"Julio, why didn't you want me to come to the lake?"

I moved closer to her, willing myself to remember her touch, her smell, her everything. I replayed in my mind the first time she appeared in my room, the times we fought to stay together while we were in Faevenly, the day we married, and the day Gabriela was born.

"Standing here with you, in your spirit form, I began to realize that if you had ended up here, and you were not in the corridor, then your body had to be here too. That somehow, Draven's magic sent your body *and* your soul to the Passing Place."

She gasped, but didn't say anything as I continued on.

"I distracted you with a request for flowers, and when you left, I searched for your body and found it not far from this spot in a field of flowers." I paused, working myself up to say the final part. "I didn't want you to know what had become of you, so I brought you here to this lake and set you in it, because I knew the cold water would preserve your body."

Her gaze pulled away from me and settled on the sparkling waters. Her mouth parted as she studied the clear blue with tiny rippling waves. "The water is cold? And I am in there?"

"It is very cold; and yes, you are in it."

She moved from the grassy area to the sand. "Will you show me?"

I nodded, then sloshed into the water, and she followed. I didn't have to go far to see her. She was submerged just under the water in the shallow part close to the riverbed. Her long silver hair and her silky blue dress drifted with the current, looking ethereal and magical.

She placed her fingertips on her lips and muttered, "stars above."

I wiped the fresh tears from my eyes, doing my best to stay calm. "Your body will stay forever in this magical place, never aging, never deteriorating. And when I die, I will come back here and see you before I join you in the horizon where the horses take the trailers with the bodies."

She swept her gaze away from the water and stared at the horizon. "I have to go there now, I think."

"I think so."

We left the river in silence, passed the creek in silence, and walked to the meadow in silence. Back in our usual spot, surrounded by lush grass and lavender flowers, she sighed. She reached out for my hands.

"My heart hurts to be leaving you, but I take comfort in knowing we will be reunited one day."

"We will."

"But not soon," she added with a look of determination. "You must go back and find Gabriela, for there is a very important task that must be completed."

"Kill Draven," we said at the same time.

25

GABRIELA

R ook and I crouched in the brush at the far end of the Strong Haven garden, in the wild area beyond the manicured hedges. Adrius and Verona had been dispatched to take out the guards, and Lady Sonia and Uncle Manny were somewhere near the front of the palace.

Leaf was inside. Or so we hoped.

We had agreed on a whistle from Adrius to alert us when it was safe to make our move. But it seemed to be taking a really long time.

"Do you think something happened to them?" I whispered.

"They are highly skilled," Rook said. "Be patient."

Patience was not one of my strengths. To keep myself distracted, I rehearsed our plan in my mind. Climb the lattice, slip through my window, creep into the large bedchamber, hope Draven was there, and slam my mouth over his.

Thinking about being that close to him made me shudder.

A low whistle sounded in three short bursts,

followed by one high trill. My stomach flipped and goose bumps raced across my skin. "That's the signal."

"Come on," Rook urged.

We emerged from our hiding spot, taking careful yet quick steps. I stayed close behind Rook, shadowing each movement, holding my breath tight. When we reached the spot where the lattice should have been, I saw only thick, bushy vines. The lattice must've been buried underneath, which meant the climb wouldn't be easy.

Rook waved me in front of him, urging me to go first. With no footholds, I shoved my boots between the leaves and clasped my hands around the growth, the vines scraping and cutting my skin. Grunting and pulling, I painstakingly scaled my way to my window, heaved myself over the ledge, and dropped in with a soft thump.

Surprisingly, Rook stayed quieter than me, pouncing through the window like a cat. Or a big puma. Working to catch my breath and rubbing my sweaty and bloodied hands on my pants, I waited a few seconds before nodding to indicate we could move to the door.

Rook patted my shoulder and eased around me. He wrapped his fingers around the doorknob, turned slowly, and nudged it ajar. Two seconds later, he swung it all the way open. The orbs that floated along the ceiling were dimmed low, casting an orange haze along the corridor, like candlelight. After a quick scan, he motioned me to follow and we filtered over the threshold.

Holding his position, Rook unsheathed his dagger, while I took my stick from my back with a tight grip. I motioned to the other end of the corridor, signaling our path, and we hurried forward. We passed the washroom; the room that belonged to my mother's sister, Malena; and the library. When we reached the marble staircase, we hugged the perimeter and kept going, until we made it to the wing with the biggest bedchamber, befitting kings and queens.

And now, Draven.

Standing before the massive wooden door carved all over with flowering vines, I imagined the deadly witch on the other side. Shivers raced down my spine. My heart slammed against my chest. My hands grew slick around my fighting stick. I kept telling myself I was fearless and powerful and that I could do anything... including sucking Draven's soul into my mouth.

Rook threw me a hard look, as if telling me to focus, and I nodded with a gulp. Then, like we planned, he wrapped his hand around the doorknob, counted to three with his fingers, and charged in. I raced in behind him and made a beeline for the bed, ready to pounce, but came to a screeching halt when I neared. The purple bedspread was smooth and tucked in at the sides, the oversized pillows fluffed and lined up perfectly.

The bed was empty.

I gasped as shivers erupted all over me, gathering sharply at the back of my neck. Before I could make a move or even utter a sound, the bedroom door behind me slammed shut with a bang. I spun around and saw Draven. He stood in the shadows, dressed in all black, lurking like a predator. His pale face and sparkling eyes gleamed through the darkness.

"Looking for me?" he slithered out.

With a sharp cry, Rook charged with his dagger. I tightened my hands around my fighting stick and stormed forward too.

"**Stop!**" Draven bellowed, in a vibrating voice.

My body froze. My stick fell out of my hand. Rook stopped dead too, his dagger clanking to the floor. Draven stepped out of the shadows, his lips curled up in a sinister smile.

"Fools," he hissed. "I smelled you all the moment you stepped on palace grounds."

All?

Panic raced through me. Did he have the others? Did he have Uncle Manny? Anger boiled inside of me. If I couldn't get close enough to take Draven's soul, I'd have to use my blue aura. I'd have to send it out and kill him before he killed us.

Keeping a keen eye on my target, I turned my mind inward, focusing on what it meant to be an Avila and a Strong. I visualized my blue aura, imagining it coming out of me like lightning and striking Draven dead. But before anything could happen, a flap of Draven's cloak cut through my thoughts. He blurred, and like a fast-moving fog, zipped over to me. His cold hand clutched my chin, his fingers digging into my skin.

"I do not think so, princess," he taunted. He raised his other hand, reached out his long skinny finger, and touched my forehead. "**Sleep.**"

OPENING MY EYES ONE AFTER THE OTHER, I REALIZED MY head was hanging low, my chin touching my chest. Blinking, I looked about, recognizing the marble and gold of the Great Hall and the rich wood of the table before me. I was sitting at the head of the formal table, and I couldn't move. Leaf sat motionless to my right. On my left were Rook, Lady Sonia, Uncle Manny, Verona, and Adrius. They were motionless too, all of them like wax figures.

"Princess Gabriela," Draven said, drawing out each syllable.

Snapping my attention to his voice, I saw the evil witch. He sat across from me at the other end of the long table. His hands were placed on the wood, folded together, as if conducting a meeting.

Swallowing my fear, and thinking I had absolutely nothing to lose, I matched his tone and said, "Draven the Witch."

He let out a chuckle, then rose to his feet and took measured steps my way. "I do love your spirit, young princess. It reminds me so much of your mother. Your father too. Part of me wishes they were not dead so that they could witness your ending. But alas, they are. Lucky for you and me, though, we do have these others here to bear witness to your ultimate demise before I end them too."

I pulled at my arms and my legs, trying to make even the slightest movement, but couldn't. His magic had me, and I was defenseless. But maybe, just maybe, if I stalled, a miracle would happen and my witchy Avila skills would kick in.

"Why, Draven?" I asked. "Why are you doing this?"

He moved behind my chair, his cloak swishing behind him. He slammed his hands on the back of the armrests, yanked the chair away from the table, and spun me around. He bent down in front of me so that we were eye to eye, then studied me. Sitting so close, I could see how beautiful he was underneath all that madness. Beautiful, deadly, and completely insane.

"Because you and your vile human blood, and all the humans who have come before you, have spoiled my precious Faevenly. That is why." He stroked the tops of my hands. "After I wipe you from existence, I will do the same to the others at this table. And when that is done, I will take care of every other human blooded in Faevenly."

My mind scrambled for my next move, wondering how I could get us out of this, when Draven stepped away from me. His diamond eyes shifted in Leaf's direction. "Leaf, come."

My stomach dropped and my spine tingled. *Leaf? Why did he want Leaf?*

Leaf's chair scraped across the floor behind me. His boots thudded against the marble. He came into view and stood before me with empty eyes.

"Leaf!" I pleaded. "Wake up! Please! It's me, Gabriela!"

"Shhh," Draven whispered. He placed his finger on my lips to silence me. "I want you to hear this."

With my heart in my throat and my voice silenced, Draven stepped back. He licked his lips, then motioned at Leaf. "**End the line.**"

What?

Leaf's eyes narrowed as the deadly warrior in him sprang to life. I had seen that expression before. Had witnessed his vicious attacks. Knew full well what he was capable of.

"Leaf! No!"

He yanked his dagger from its sheath, swept in, and plunged the thick blade deep into my stomach. My mouth fell open as numbing pain shot through me. I could feel the blood draining from my body as a cold rush trickled down from my head. A convulsing gasp tore from me, followed by another, as my vision dimmed and my eyes closed.

"Gabriela, *mija*," a voice called out in a hurry. "Wake up. Wake up. "

My eyes snapped open and I gasped for air, my

hands shooting to my stomach. But instead of meeting flesh and blood, they went right through me.

"Gabriela," a different voice said. "Focus. We are right here."

I blinked once, and then again, as everything around me came into view. My mom and dad were kneeling beside me. All around us sprawled lush green grass, bright blooming flowers, and the most magnificent sparkly blue sky.

I was in the Passing Place.

"Oh no," I muttered, sitting up. "I'm... dead."

Mom and Dad looked at each other with fire and determination, then back at me.

"Not for long," my dad rushed out. "We need to get you back to your body, right now, before it's too late."

They stood, and I did too. Still stunned and in a daze, I worked to process my dad's words. "Before it's too late?"

"Yes, you need to get back while your body is still able to receive you," Dad said.

"Open to receiving your spiritual self," Mom explained.

Dad rubbed his gold wedding ring. A hazy bubble stretched out, becoming bigger and wider with each tug.

"There's a shimmer in your ring?" I asked. It reminded me of the one inside Lady Sonia's necklace.

Dad continued manipulating the portal, first with only one hand, then with both. "Remember how I told you, the first time you visited here, that Lady Sonia made shimmers for your mom and me, and also one for you, so that we could get to each other and you if we needed to?"

I blinked, remembering the conversation well. "Yes."

Dad continued stretching. "This is your shimmer. We're using it to go to your body. And you're putting your spirit back where it belongs."

"But... I've been stabbed." I looked down at my form. I didn't see any signs of injury or blood, not here, but in the palace I knew I was a bloody mess. "How can I return into an injured body?"

Mom reached for me, her translucent hands hovering near mine. "When you get back, you need to step into your body. The magic of being in this place should make you whole again. But only if you hurry."

She brought her face close to mine, as if kissing my cheek. Then she did the same to Dad. With purpose in her eyes, and wearing a brave face, she waved us toward the shimmer. "Go, go."

"Mom," I choked out, not wanting to leave her and finally understanding why my dad had stayed with her. "I love you."

"I love you, my beautiful girl. Always and forever." She drifted closer to my dad. "I love you, Julio. With everything."

"I love you more than that," he said.

"Not possible," she said with a smile. "Now hurry!"

With one final look at my mom, I stepped through the haze and into the Great Hall. I scanned the scene quickly. My bloodied body was slumped over in my chair. Draven was still standing in front of me with Leaf at his side, but now he was taunting the others. I had no idea if he could see me, or what my dad was going to do when he passed through behind me.

All I knew was what I needed to do.

I darted to the chair and lowered my otherworldly self into my corporeal being. I stayed there, eyes closed, willing myself to heal, waiting for the magic of the Passing Place to do whatever it needed to do.

Tingles prickled my scalp, then flowed down from my head to my toes. A pleasing warmth swirled in my stomach, small at first then grew until it filled me. I twitched my fingers, followed by my toes. Then, seething with anger, I leapt out of my seat and barreled into Draven. We crashed to the floor in a heap, face to face. His eyes went wide as I slammed my mouth over his thin, cold lips, unleashing my soul vamp self.

Like Lady Sonia had said, my instincts kicked in.

I drew a long, shaking breath, my body alive with a hunger that wasn't entirely my own. The pull began low in my chest—dark, primal, unstoppable—and then his soul tore free. It hit me in a rush, pouring into me like smoke and fire. The taste of it was sharp, metallic, electric. His screams echoed inside my head as his essence flooded my taste buds, bitter and sweet all at once.

Then I felt the others. Hundreds of them. Thousands.

They surged through him in a torrent, screaming

and whispering, clawing their way free as I gulped them in. The air around us spiraled into a violent current, whipping my hair across my face, filling my lungs with the taste of ash and memory.

I couldn't stop. Didn't want to.

I drew harder, devouring every last wisp, until the shadows that made up Draven unraveled, and there was nothing left of the witch but silence.

A feeling of bliss and satisfaction set in, letting me know I was finished. I sat back, in awe and shock over what I had done, staring down at Draven's shriveled body. But then he moved. His face twitched. His shriveled mouth smiled and he managed a final utterance.

"Kill me, kill him."

His eyes rolled back and his head dropped to the side. Shouting filled the room.

"Leaf!" Rook yelled.

Only then did I feel my dad's hands on my shoulders. He was pulling me off of Draven's corpse because something was horribly wrong. I scrambled to my feet and turned to see Leaf on the ground, lifeless.

I dashed over to him and fell to my knees, my hands shaking as I brought them to his face. "No, no, no," I cried, realizing the witch had somehow linked their souls. I raised my watery stare to Lady Sonia. "There has to be a way to save him."

She pursed her lips in concentration, then nodded. "You can give him half of your soul and revive him. If you do that, you will be linked forever. Your death will mean his death, and his will mean yours."

My dad knelt next to me. I faced him, praying he could help me figure out what to do. He always knew what to do. "Dad, what do I do?"

He placed his hand on mine and squeezed. "Do what your heart is telling you to do."

My heart.

Looking down at Leaf, I thought of everything he was—complicated, angry, tender, fierce, loyal, and completely mine. I studied his beautiful face and placed my hand on his cheek. He had my heart in every way. If I could save him, I had to. He was my future, and I never wanted to be away from him.

I leaned over and kissed him. Keeping my lips on his, I opened my mouth slightly, the movement opening his too. While joined together, I concentrated on his life, willing mine to revive his. I thought of the way he looked at me, the times he touched me, the fierce protectiveness he had over me. All the moments we had shared tumbled together in my mind while a soft wisp of air gathered inside of me. It wasn't forceful or angry, but easy and light, and filled with tenderness, warmth, and intimacy. The pleasing swirl flowed out of my mouth and into his. When it left in a puff, I sat back.

Leaf stayed still. I was beginning to think that what I had done wasn't working, when his chest moved up, then down, and his breath began flowing freely. It took a few more seconds for his eyes to open.

He blinked. "Gabriela?"

"Yes, it's me."

He sat up all the way with a bewildered expression painted on his face. He scanned the room and saw the others. My dad reached over and patted him on the back.

"Welcome back, Leaf."

Leaf tilted his head at my dad, and then me, and then back at my dad. "Welcome back to you, as well, Lord Julio."

With a nod, my dad left me and Leaf together, then shooed everyone away. I had a lot to tell Leaf, and I was sure he had a lot to tell me, but all of that could wait. He must've felt the same, because neither one of us said anything as we threw our arms around each other and held on tight.

26

GABRIELA

Voices and footsteps sounded in the corridor, pulling me and Leaf apart. With a frown, he rose to his feet and helped me to mine.

"What now?" he muttered.

"Please let it be nothing awful," I said. "I can't take more awful."

Uncle Leto and a handful of guards swept into the Great Hall. My dad and the others were with them, and I let out a sigh of relief. The tall and imposing fae wore a scowl and took long strides to the spot where Draven lay. He stopped and narrowed his stare on the shriveled witch, then nudged him with his boot.

With no response from Draven, he said, "Faevenly is finally rid of Draven." Moving away from the body, he came over to me. "My princess, I have already offered my apologies to the others for my delay. Now I offer the same to you. We got here as soon as we could."

"It's okay, Uncle Leto," I said, grateful to see him. "We managed."

His brow shot up as he scanned my bloodied

clothes. "I should say so, and I would very much like to hear what transpired here. But first, we must secure the palace." He turned and called to his men. "Check every nook and cranny of the palace. Bring me any who stand with Draven, kill those who show resistance."

"I will help," Verona volunteered.

"As will I," Adrius added.

They took off, leaving me and Leaf with my dad, Uncle Leto, Uncle Manny, Lady Sonia, and Rook. We gathered around Draven's body and stood in silence for a while. I still couldn't believe he was really dead.

"What do we do with him?" I asked.

"Burn him," Uncle Leto said. "Immediately. When the guards finish their sweep, we can have them prepare a pyre."

"Sounds good to me," Leaf said.

"The sooner the better," Uncle Manny chimed in with a shudder.

My dad flashed Uncle Manny a curious look, and Uncle Manny shrugged. "It's a long story."

"I can only imagine," my dad said, clapping his best friend on the back.

"I would like to hear that tale as well, but for now, let us get away from this filth," Uncle Leto said.

We moved away from Draven's body and gathered at the far end of the room, standing in a tight circle. Lady Sonia spoke. "There is another matter to address. We cannot forget that Draven threatened all the humans in Faevenly. He mentioned it in this very room, and Majestic the sprite also shared the information."

I placed my hand on my stomach against my bloodstained shirt. I had been so focused on ending Draven, I had forgotten about his threats.

"That's right," I said. "Does anyone have any idea what he meant?"

"I do," Leaf offered. "With Draven dead, and my compulsion erased, I remember everything he said and did to me. He means to use the waterways to kill all the humans in this realm."

"Thunderation," Uncle Leto spat. "We must act quickly." He pointed at Rook and Uncle Manny. "You two, come with me to Torch Lake. The rest of you, accompany Lady Sonia to check the potion room and the healing chamber."

"Just the healing chamber," Lady Sonia said to us as we headed in different directions. "No one can find, let alone access, my potion room."

Remembering all the times I spent looking for that room and never finding it, I knew she was right.

We hustled out of the Great Hall, down the corridor, and past the cook house and to the healing chamber. When we stepped in, we practically froze.

On the wooden table in the middle of the room sat a large jar about the size of a small aquarium, and inside floated a massive chunk of aquoise.

"The aquoise," I whispered.

The stone wasn't blue anymore; it was red with

blue streaks. Jagged spires jutted out at every angle, in a starburst pattern. The water matched the stone in hue, and as we got closer, the smell of dead animals wafted our way.

"Holy hell," my dad uttered, covering his mouth. "What is that thing?"

Lady Sonia covered her mouth and stepped closer. She circled the table, studying the rock. "A potion, made with the aquoise and who knows what other ingredients."

Holding my arm over my mouth, I moved closer to Leaf, found his hand, and held on tight. "What was Draven going to do with it?"

"I imagine his plan was to empty it into Torch Lake," Lady Sonia answered, still studying the rock.

"It must be destroyed," Leaf said.

"I agree," my dad chimed in. "But how?"

Lady Sonia kept circling. "I do not know the composition nor the power of the liquid, but I think we can all agree that the liquid and the stone cannot make contact with anything. Not the waters, not the soil, not the grass, not even our skin. It is too dangerous."

"How do we manage that if we need to get rid of this thing?" Leaf asked.

My churning mind went to a drought we had in Texas a few years ago. It was so bad the creeks and ponds dried up. Even Lake Travis was so low we couldn't use our boat. I turned to my dad. "It needs to be evaporated. Like a drought."

"Good thinking, my girl," he said. "It's the only way."

"But how can such a thing be accomplished?" Lady Sonia asked.

Keeping my attention on my dad, I thought of our witchy Avila skills. He must've thought the same thing. "We can do it, *mija*."

Feeling strong and powerful, I thought he was right. "Absolutely, we can."

Leaf squeezed my hand, then let go and stepped back. Lady Sonia moved away too, while my dad and I advanced forward. We positioned ourselves at opposite ends of the table. He placed his hands on the glass, and I placed mine on the other side.

"Concentrate on your light, *mija*. Envision it flowing from you like a powerful wind. Imagine it hot, like the brightest sun."

"So it can dry up what's inside the jar," I finished.

"That's right."

He closed his eyes, and I closed mine. Doing what he said, I pictured my blue power coming out of me. But instead of wind, only the image of the sun sprang to mind—huge, spinning, glowing, and blazing hot. I envisioned my aura like that, powerful and deadly, capable of scorching the glass jar with a blast, burning the water and the stone, turning them to a crisp. Immersed in my thoughts, I started feeling a warm glow all around me. It was pleasing and comforting, reminding me of the feeling when you step out of the shadows and into the sunlight.

"Gabriela," a voice said. Soft at first, it felt like a tickle. "Gabriela," it said again, this time louder, like a bell. "Gabriela!" it screamed, rushing at me like an explosion.

My eyes snapped open, and the scene sprang into view. Leaf's arms were locked around my waist, his face buried in the nook of my neck as he pulled me back from the table. My dad and Lady Sonia stood near the wall, shielding their eyes from the light. The rotten stench had vanished, replaced by the clean, sharp scents of peppermint, eucalyptus, and vanilla. The glass jar was gone—so was the liquid. And in its place, the aquoise stone hovered in midair, bathed in blue, sparkling like a brilliant star that blinded everyone in the room but me.

It called to me—softly at first, like a whisper in my soul—until I realized the light wasn't just shining *for* me. It was *reaching* for me.

My dad kept his hands up, shielding his eyes. "The power is coming from you!" he shouted. "Power it down!"

Raising my hands, I saw a blue hue floating all over me, like a magic second layer of skin. He was right. The power was coming from me and I needed to stop it before everyone in the room was obliterated.

Keeping a sharp eye on the aquoise, I kept my hands up, my palms facing out, and repeated over and over in my mind, *power down, power down, power down*.

Ever so slowly, the dazzling rock grew smaller and smaller until all that remained was a tiny shard of blue that resembled a snowflake. Everyone lowered their hands, watching the flake in awe, wondering what to do next, when it zipped over to me and flew into my chest.

My hands flew to the spot. "Oh my gosh," I uttered, shuffling back, a feeling like a cool burst of air filling my lungs. "W-w-what just happened?"

Lady Sonia moved close. She narrowed her eyes and placed her hand on my forehead. She held it there for a few long seconds, then lowered her arm. "I do not sense any harm, or any danger, but... that last remaining piece of aquoise is in you now."

Dad swept in. "Can you remove it?" he asked Lady Sonia.

She shook her head. "I cannot. It has chosen her, and there it will remain."

"Until when?" Leaf asked, his voice laced with worry.

"Until it wants to leave, I suppose," she answered.

Terror filled me, and even though Lady Sonia had said it was harmless, I wasn't so sure. "That remnant of aquoise was made by Draven for a spell to kill humans, and I'm mostly human. So having that in me can't be good. Right?"

"It is not anything," Lady Sonia said. "It is not good; it is not bad. But if it will make you feel better, I can look into it and see if there is a way to remove it."

I blew out. "Yes, that would make me feel a lot better."

"Me too," my dad said.

Then she added an afterthought. "Let us keep this to ourselves, until I know more."

My dad raised his brow at me, letting me know it was up to me to decide if we should keep it quiet. With a slight shrug, thinking it was probably a good thing nobody knew about the potentially deadly magic inside of me, I said, "That actually sounds wise."

Leto, Rook, and Uncle Manny entered the potion chamber, missing everything that had happened by mere seconds.

"We have completed our inspection of Torch Lake and, other than the shimmers being destroyed, we found nothing amiss," Leto said. "What of you all?"

Lady Sonia was quick to serve as our mouthpiece. "We discovered a potion Draven had been concocting with the aquoise. Lady Gabriela and Lord Julio eliminated it with their magic."

Uncle Manny clapped his hands. "Good job!" His eyes were wide with hope. "Does that mean this whole disaster is over? Once and for all?"

A hint of doubt crept inside of me, but I didn't let it show. Instead, I chose to hold on to the hope that everything was, indeed, over. It was better than the alternative.

"Yes," I said, with the best smile I could muster. "This whole disaster is over."

My dad, Uncle Leto, Uncle Manny, Leaf, Lady Sonia, Rook, and I planned our next move. Not just for us, but for all of Faevenly.

We sat outside on the patio at the large table where we always had breakfast when we visited. A soft breeze filtered around us, carrying with it smells of jasmine, rose, and gardenia. Birds sang and large butterflies the size of my hands darted about. You would never have known that off in the wild part of the palace grounds, we had just burned Draven.

Signs of weariness shadowed Leaf's eyes as he shifted in his seat. No doubt, he needed a long bath and peaceful rest, like the rest of us. But not yet. We had stuff to decide.

"What now, Lord Julio and Princess Gabriela?" Uncle Leto asked. "What plans do you have for yourselves and for Strong Haven?"

My dad tapped the table for a bit before raising his eyes and meeting my gaze. "I will stand with my daughter, either here in Faevenly or back in the human realm. The shimmers of Torch Lake are gone, but I still have mine, and I'm prepared to do whatever she wants."

Leaf sat beside me, and I didn't have to look at him to feel his mood shift as he waited for my answer. He wanted me to stay.

Sitting a little taller, I cleared my throat, my thoughts about Faevenly coming into focus quickly because I had already been thinking about what I wanted to do if we came out of this alive.

"I know I haven't spent much time here. I know how dangerous this realm is. But I love Faevenly and Strong Haven. I've never felt more myself than I do when I'm here." I shifted my body toward my dad, giving him my full attention. "So, if you're sure it's okay, I'd like to stay."

He smiled and took my hand. "It's okay with me. We do need to go back, though, and tell *Abuela* and tie up some loose ends before we move here permanently."

"But we can visit with your shimmer whenever we want," I added. "Right?"

"Of course we can."

Uncle Leto beamed. "Strong Haven will be most pleased to have a Strong back in the palace."

"I will be pleased, as well," Lady Sonia said.

"As will the Sublands," Rook said, pounding his fist against the table.

"Um, what about me?" Uncle Manny asked.

My dad chuckled. "What about you?"

"Hey, now," Uncle Manny said, punching my dad's shoulder.

"I'm kidding, Manny," my dad said with a punch back. But then he took on a serious expression. "What would you like to do? If you want, you can stay here with us. We'd love to have you."

He laughed, then said, "Uh, stay in a world with dangerous fast horses, spells and potions, with angry fae and potential for war at any given moment?" He paused, then grinned, "Why not?" He rubbed his face.

"Besides, it's not like I can go back looking like this, anyway." He raised a questioning brow at Lady Sonia. "Is this"—he waved at his youthful body—"permanent? I'd actually like to keep this and get older from here on if possible."

She nodded. "As far as I can tell, you will age from this point forward."

He wiped his brow. "Phew, that's good to hear. I've got some things I'd like to do-over in my life, and now I have the chance."

Dad reached over and grasped his shoulder. "I'm happy for you, Manny."

Then Uncle Manny joked, "Can I call you dad?"

"No."

Everyone had a good laugh, but when the chuckling died down, Uncle Leto turned the discussion back to official business. "With all that decided, I will dispatch ravens alerting the other provinces that Draven the Witch is dead and announcing the return of Lord Julio and Princess Gabriela to Strong Haven."

"We should dispatch a troop to High Meadow as well," Rook suggested. " I do not think the Kanes will take the news lightly."

Uncle Leto rubbed his chin. "You are right." He pushed himself away from the table and rose to his feet. "Let us see to our matters, then."

"I'll be back, *mija*," my dad said, joining Uncle Leto.

Everyone went to their tasks, and finally, I was alone with Leaf.

He reached out and grabbed my hands and pulled me to him. "I am glad you are staying."

Gazing into his amazing blue eyes, I said, "I am too."

He traced my face with his fingers, then kissed me. With my heart soaring and my head in the clouds, I knew that whatever happened from here, I would always be with him, and he would always be with me.

And somehow, we would all be fine.

EPILOGUE

S itting on the ledge of my window, breathing in the cool and crisp nighttime air and watching the brilliant stars overhead, I still couldn't believe my dad, Uncle Manny, and I lived in Faevenly now, in the Strong Haven Palace.

We had moved six months ago with only a few suitcases of clothes. We left our other stuff behind, because we really didn't need anything else. Not that we needed human clothes, but I still wanted some of my shoes, my jeans, my favorite T-shirts. If we needed anything else, we could always use my dad's shimmer to get it.

But we didn't use the shimmer often. Not anymore. *Abuela* was adjusting well to us living over here. Plus, she had the rest of the family to look in on her. But I sure did miss her and her cooking. My dad, Manny, and I could never really replicate her recipes.

A soft knock at the door pulled me away from my thoughts. "Come in."

Maid Gidna swept into the room with my evening tray of water, fruit, and oils. "Good evening, princess."

"Good evening, Maid Gidna."

She set the tray on the table by my bed, then got busy with what I referred to as her turn-down service. At first, I told her I didn't need my bedsheets pulled down or a tray brought in or a mist sprayed. But she insisted. So I let her. Plus, I loved the company.

Getting up off my perch, I joined her on the other side of the king-sized bed. We removed the excess pillows, then pulled down the soft silk sheets and fluffy feathered bedspread.

"Anything new today?" I asked, as she moved on to spritzing the room with lavender.

Strong Haven Palace was quiet. Especially with the newly signed peace agreement between the provinces. But every now and again, there would be some news to report.

She looked up, as if searching her mind. "Oh, yes! We received a large shipment of peaches today from Lady Wren. They are ripe and delicious, and I even put some on your evening tray."

My mouth watered as I glanced at the assortment she had brought in. "Sounds yummy. Thank you."

"Lady Wren also sent word of the birth of a litter of wolfbeasts!" she exclaimed, beaming. "Ten in all!"

"Really? Do you think I can have one?" The wolfbeasts were bound to the Strongs, but they stayed deep in Strong Haven's western lands. I had yet to see one.

"I do not see why not. You must ask your father tomorrow when he and your uncle return from Sand Bluff," she said with a firm nod.

"Good idea."

With the bed and spritzing finished, Maid Gidna folded her hands in front of her. "Will there be anything else, Princess?"

"Nothing else. Thank you, Gidna."

She offered me a slight bow of her head. "See you in the morning, Princess."

Scooping up the tray, I plopped on my bed and started eating the peaches, plums, and berries, and sipping my rose-flavored water that contained a droplet of a serum Lady Sonia had prepared to make me age at the same rate as the fae. My dad and Uncle Manny drank the same thing every night.

When I finished, I set the tray back on the table. Feeling exhausted and ready for sleep, I was making my way to use the washroom when a tiny rock flew by me. My heart warmed, and I rushed over to the window as Leaf leapt in. He strode toward me, hooked his arm around my waist, and pulled me to him.

"Hello, my princess."

I slipped my hands behind his neck and lifted myself up on my toes. "Hello, my fae warrior."

He parted his lips, then pressed them against mine, kissing me with so much passion I couldn't feel the floor beneath my feet.

"Mmm," he said, as we slowly separated. "I long for the day when we can always be together."

My dad had insisted Leaf and I wait a year before we formally declared our intention to bind ourselves to one another. He wanted me to get to know Leaf better as well as settle into my new role as an official princess. His logic made sense, so I agreed. But it was getting harder and harder to be away from Leaf.

"I know," I sighed. "But a year will go by before we know it."

Gazing at me with aching passion, he swept me up in his arms and walked me over to my bed. "I will gladly wait a year for our formal declaration, but I cannot wait another minute before I can ravish you again."

Shivers of excitement and desire raced across my skin, because I didn't want to wait either. With the late hour and with Maid Gidna gone, and my dad and uncle away, I was sure no one would bother us.

"Well, then," I breathed. "Don't wait."

We crashed onto the bed, ripping each other's clothes off, kissing, touching, and loving throughout the night. When there was nothing else to give, we stayed close, our legs intertwined and our bodies pressed together.

"I love you," he said against my ear as he stroked my back. "With all of me."

With a squeeze, I said back, "I love you, with all of me."

With a deep sigh, I closed my eyes and snuggled into him, knowing he'd be up and out of my room before daylight, but taking whatever I could from him before he left.

Drifting off in the most contented exhaustion, I was

almost asleep when a pulling sensation overcame me, followed by a dip of weightlessness.

I bolted upright with a start, trying to catch my balance when I found myself in a bright space. I shielded my eyes, blinking for a few seconds, then slowly lowered my hands.

Instead of seeing my bed, or Leaf, or my bedchamber, I saw sparkling lake waters. The cool ripples lapped against my ankles as a soft breeze swept over me, ruffling the bottom of a long white gown that hung from my body, even though moments earlier I wasn't wearing anything.

"I must be dreaming," I murmured. "But why am I alone in a lake?"

"You are not alone," a melodic voice said.

The comforting words beckoned to me, ringing magical and familiar. As I stepped forward, a flowing blue silk dress came into view beneath the water, as did my mother's beautiful face.

"Mom!" I called out, edging as close to her body as I could.

She smiled, her green eyes sparkling with joy to see me, but then quickly took on a grave expression. "My beautiful Gabriela. I have brought you here to warn you of a dark future."

Even though she spoke underwater, I could hear her as if she stood beside me. "In the coming years, peace will cease to exist in Faevenly. One generation hence, a child will be born unto our bloodline who will fight to restore it. You must prepare this land for that child's arrival."

Shock took my words and all I could do was stare at her, open-mouthed and afraid. "But... what do I do?"

"You will know."

A buzzing sound circled my head, turning my attention away from my mother. Looking up, I saw the tiny brown body and gold wings of Majestic. She soared down to me, then hovered within inches of my face.

"Oh, Princess, oh Princess. I am frightened for the future. So very frightened."

I held out my palm, and she landed on my skin with a soft tickle. She clasped her hands together in front of her, blinking at me with long gold lashes.

"I am too," I said to her in a whisper.

A dizzy feeling twirled in my stomach, whisking me away and pulling me from Majestic and the lake in a blur. With a kick of my legs, my body jerked and my eyes flew open.

Leaf wrapped his arm around me and pulled me close. "Gabriela? Are you all right? You are trembling."

My breath came out in short panicked bursts as my heart slammed against my chest. I pushed my long hair away from my face. "I just had the strangest dream."

He lifted himself up on his elbow. The dim orb overhead in the corner of the room glowed behind him, showcasing his chiseled face and muscular body. "What was it?"

A warning? A prophecy? Or me just being paranoid? I didn't know, but I was tired of being afraid. I placed my hand on the cross that hung around my neck, saying a quick prayer for everything to be okay, then pulled Leaf close to me.

"It was nothing."

AS SLEEP FINALLY CLAIMED ME, SOMETHING DEEP WITHIN stirred—quiet, restless, and waiting. As though the peace we had fought so hard to claim was only the beginning... and something far greater had yet to come.

And somehow, I knew the future would demand more from us than we had ever imagined.

CONCLUSION OF BOOK FOUR

The battle is over.
But the cost will echo forever.

A new journey begins in *A Storm Rises*.
Because not every ending is what it seems.

A new destiny unfolds... but not without sacrifice.

Start reading A Storm Rises now.

"As sure as the sun rises and falls, everything will change after the hunt."

Experience the epic twists and turns of
A Storm Rises!

FAE BLOODLINES SERIES

Fae Away, book 1

Fae Fractured, book 2

Fae Hunted, book 3

Fae Rising, book 4

For a full list of Rose Garcia's books and how each series is connected, please visit

https://www.rosegarciabooks.com/garciaverse

ACKNOWLEDGMENTS

Here it is, the end of the Fae Bloodlines Series, and I have so many emotions! Cue the tears, and pass the tissue! Somebody hold me!!

I absolutely fell in love with Celyse and Julio, and their daughter, Gabriela, as I crafted their story. And, of course, Leaf, Leto, Manny, Rook, Lady Sonia, *Abuela*, and the rest of the gang. And Jaid, oh, Jaid! Why did I do that to you??

For four books, I've been eating, sleeping, and dreaming about these characters and all their ups and downs. I'm going to miss them so very much! I hope you will miss them too!

I have so many people to thank who've helped me and stood by me during this incredible journey. First and foremost, I have to give thanks to God for keeping me and my family safe and healthy. Next, a HUGE thanks to my husband and my two kids for supporting me as I've journeyed through my fae world. Especially my husband who's helped me work my way through all kinds of writer's block. He has earned the title of Creative Director and Patient Husband. He's the bestest!

To my incredible tried and true, ride or die, with

me from the very beginning, friend and beta reader, Jessica Ramirez! You are such a huge blessing to me and I'm so very grateful for you! Thank you so very much for believing in me, helping me, reading my books, giving me feedback, and just being a wonderful human being!

To the fantastic PAs who've been the wind beneath my wings! To Emily Prebich who worked tirelessly with me on the release of Fae Hunted, thank you so much! And to Christine Hutton who's done so much for the release of Fae Rising, you are a total rock star! Also, a huge thanks to Gladys Gonzales Atwell for always being willing to help when needed, thank you so much!

To my incredible editor, Liz Ferry, thank you for always working around my crazy schedule! Seriously, you wake up when I go to bed. We are the dream team! Also, I'm exhausted, lol.

I am so very grateful to each and every one of my awesome readers! Thank you so much for loving my stories! A special shout out to the readers who've joined my FB fan group, the Rose Bud Society. I love my incredible Rose Buds and appreciate your love and support more than you'll ever know! Y'all are AMAZING!

Finally, to my bestie writer friends, my Queens of the Quill—you know who you are and I'm not even joking when I say your support and friendship means SO MUCH TO ME!

Now, with all that being said, upward and onward

with my next project- a sequel series to Fae Bloodlines, Bloodlines Legacy. I'm dreaming up the most incredible twist that I can't wait to unleash on you!

To keep up with what I'm doing, please subscribe to my newsletter at https://www.rosegarciabooks.com/newsletter.

What a fun journey we're on!

ABOUT THE AUTHOR

 **Rose Garcia** is a *USA Today* bestselling author and screenwriter known for crafting heart-stopping fantasy stories where belief is power, love defies all, and hope burns brightest. Magic is real in her world—and the only thing more dangerous than a broken heart... is a hopeful one.

A lawyer turned writer, Rose weaves stories of complicated romance, powerful families, deep-rooted friendships, and ancestral magic drawn from her Mexican American heritage. Her diverse heroes are driven by bold hearts, forced to confront tangled destinies and make impossible choices.

When she's not writing, you can find her designing escape rooms for her husband, obsessing over fantasy shows, traveling, or hanging out with her three needy and precious rescue dogs.

Rose lives in Houston, Texas, and believes tacos are a core food group—because well, they are.

For more on Rose, visit www.rosegarciabooks.com.

A final request: please review her books and spread the word about her stories. She would be most appreciative!

Join Rose's Facebook Fan Group!
www.facebook.com/groups/TheRoseBudSociety

Subscribe to Rose's Newsletter!
www.rosegarciabooks.com/newsletter